50 STATES

OUR AMERICA

Editor, TIME For Kids: Nellie Gonzalez Cutler
Senior Editor, TIME For Kids: Brenda Iasevoli

LIBERTY
STREET

Executive Editor: Beth Sutinis
Project Editors: Nicole Fisher and Deirdre Langeland
Art Director: Georgia Morrissey
Designer: Laura Klynstra
Production Manager: Hillary Leary
Prepress Manager: Alex Voznesenskiy

Published by Liberty Street, an imprint of Time Inc. Books
225 Liberty Street
New York, NY 10281

ISBN: 978-1-68330-006-9
Library of Congress Control Number: 2016960592

First edition, 2017
1 QGT 17
10 9 8 7 6 5 4 3 2 1

Some of the content in this book was originally published in TIME For Kids: *Our 50 United States and Other U.S. Lands*

We welcome your comments and suggestions about Time Inc. Books.
Please write to us at:

Time Inc. Books
Attention: Book Editors
P.O. Box 62310
Tampa, FL 33662-2310
(800) 765-6400

timeincbooks.com

Time Inc. Books products may be purchased for business or promotional use. For information on bulk purchases, please contact Christi Crowley in the Special Sales Department at (845) 895-9858.

50 STATES
OUR AMERICA

By the editors of *TIME FOR KIDS* magazine

with John H. Maher III

Illustrations by Aaron Meshon

Contents

OTHER U.S. LANDS

REGIONS

Tribal Nations Before European Settlement

For thousands of years before the continent we now call North America was colonized by Europeans, many, many different tribal nations lived here. Most historians believe that humans first came to America from Asia during the last ice age, as many as 16,000 years ago.

The people of these tribal nations are sometimes called the indigenous peoples of the Americas and are other times referred to as Native Americans or American Indians. While there are a number of different terms that continue to be debated today, it is best to refer to each tribal group by its own name.

Some of the most powerful and influential tribes today make their homes on reservations, where they live mostly by their own laws. But many of these tribes once claimed territories that were very different from where they live today.

This map of Indian nations was published in an atlas in 1893. Like many historical maps, it is not a perfect representation. But it does show the diversity of tribal groups in the lands that would become the United States. The colored boxes call out some well-known groups.

The **PUEBLO** people, native to the Southwest, built homes of stone and a clay brick called adobe. These complex structures were sometimes built into cliffsides and often resembled modern apartment buildings.

The **APACHE**, who were native to the Southwestern U.S., were considered fearsome warriors by the U.S. Army.

The **SIOUX** peoples were originally from lands around the source of the Mississippi River but have lived on the Great Plains since the 1700s. The Sioux peoples included a number of related tribes, and are categorized into three major groups—the Dakota, Lakota, and Nakota peoples.

The **IROQUOIS**, forest-dwelling people whose land spanned much of the Northeast, were five to six tribes, or nations, that had made a pact to work together. Historians believe that this model, called a confederacy, might have influenced the Founding Fathers of the United States when they considered types of government to replace English rule.

The **MISSISSIPPIAN** people built massive flat-topped dirt mounds near the Mississippi River. At its height, the Mississippian culture had a larger population than any settler city in America did until the 1800s.

The **CHEROKEE** were originally from the Southeastern U.S. but relocated to Oklahoma during the presidency of Andrew Jackson. They were one of the first tribes to become citizens of the U.S.

The **SHOSHONE** people, also called the Snake Nation, lived around the Rocky Mountains. To the west of the Rocky Mountains, the Shoshone lived in grass huts, hunted small game, and fished. To the east, the Shoshones hunted buffalo and lived in tepees.

European Settlement

In the 1400s, European nations were locked in a race for power. Countries such as France, Spain, England, and Portugal began to explore the parts of the world that were unknown to them. The countries wanted to be the first to discover new territories. They also wanted to gain wealth from trade and, eventually, to conquer those territories for themselves.

One of the European explorers who sailed at this time, Christopher Columbus, is known for "discovering" America in 1492. However, historians believe that a Viking explorer named Leif Eriksson had reached the Americas 500 years before Columbus arrived.

The first British colony—and the beginning of the U.S. as we know it—was established in 1607 by a group of nearly 100 men and boys looking for treasure, especially gold. Called Jamestown, the settlement was located in what is now the state of Virginia.

Life was hard for the early settlers. To reach the new continent, they had to make a 3,000-mile journey in cramped wooden ships. The dangerous Atlantic Ocean crossing took five months. Once settlers reached America, things only got harder. The plants and animals of the New World were strange to them. At first, they had a hard time finding enough to eat, and many got very sick or died from lack of food.

Soon, the Jamestown settlers made contact with a local indigenous tribe, called the Powhatan. At first, the Powhatan gave food to the settlers, but eventually fights broke out over who owned the land and the plants and animals that lived on it. The

Pilgrims at Plymouth Rock, on the coast of what became Massachusetts, 1620

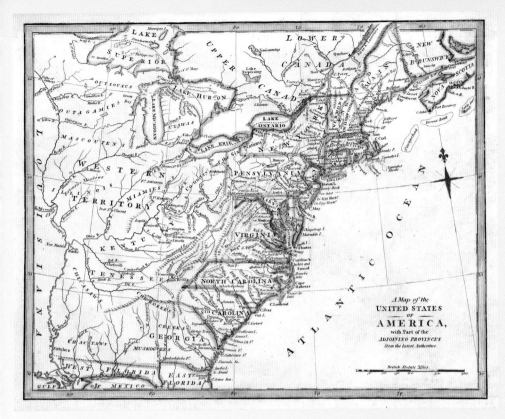

Map showing the United States in 1795

settlers and the Powhatan fought for hundreds of years. In 1608, a boatload of new settlers, including women, arrived, and families began to pop up. The settlement became a colony of Great Britain—a land ruled by the king of England.

Other early settlers of America were members of a religious group known as the Puritans, seeking a land where they could practice their religion in peace after the king of England began to persecute them for their faith. We call these people Pilgrims. The Pilgrims landed in 1620 in what is now Massachusetts, traveling on a ship called the *Mayflower*.

After years of being ruled by the king of England from thousands of miles away, the American colonists began to feel angry that they were forced to pay taxes—money owed to a government—on goods like stamps, sugar, and tea. The colonists were also angry that they were not allowed to send representatives to vote in the British Parliament. After King George III of England refused to change his mind on taxes and representation, the colonists rebelled. In 1776, they declared their independence from Britain. After the American Revolution, the 13 British colonies became the United States of America.

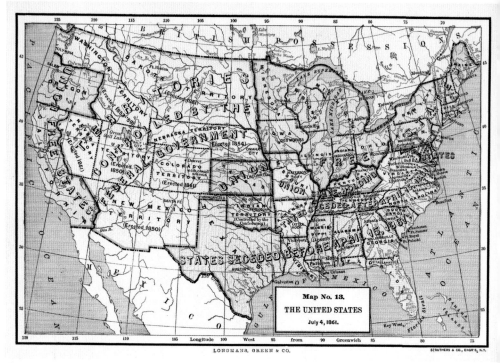

The United States, July 4, 1861

Westward Expansion

In the middle of the 19th century, the American journalist John L. O'Sullivan wrote that America should annex—or claim as its own—what was then the Republic of Texas. O'Sullivan argued that the U.S. had been chosen by God to spread democracy across the entire North American continent and that because of this, it had the right to control that continent. He called this idea Manifest Destiny.

The American government agreed. During the 150 years following the American Revolution, the country expanded to three times its original size. By 1959, the original 13 states had grown to the 50 we know today. Sometimes presidents made deals with the rulers of other countries to gain land. Thomas Jefferson bought around 828,000 square miles of land from Napoléon Bonaparte, the emperor of France, as part of the Louisiana Purchase. Other times, the U.S. waged war with another country and seized land by force. America gained the land that now makes up New Mexico, Arizona, Utah, Nevada, and the southern part of California in the Mexican-American War.

It would be many years before settlers made their way to the new lands. When Americans first set off in large groups from the eastern side of the continent to live in the West, they often did so in search of farmable land or gold. The famous Gold Rush in 1848 and 1849 brought more than 300,000 people to what is now the state of California after a worker at a lumber mill found gold in the water nearby. After the government passed the Homestead Act of 1862, which gave away millions of acres of empty land to aspiring farmers at little to no cost, many also traveled to the Great Plains to start farms.

All this expansion came at the expense of the American Indians who had lived on those lands for thousands of years. The indigenous peoples of the Americas did not have nations with defined borders like those in Europe—the sort of nations that the citizens of the U.S. were used to. Americans felt free to take territory from the tribal nations, pushing them away to new territories or forcing them onto small reservations, entirely changing their ways of life.

Sometimes, the U.S. acquired this land by signing treaties. More often, the land was acquired through forced occupation and war. The campaigns against the indigenous peoples of the Americas lasted for hundreds of years. Historians estimate that before Europeans settled America, the population of tribal nations in what is now the U.S. might have been as high as 100 million people. Today, the population of the indigenous peoples is about 5.4 million.

American Indians greet explorers Meriwether Lewis and William Clark after the two crossed a river on the frontier.

The United States Today

WASHINGTON

OREGON

MONTANA

NORTH DAKOTA

IDAHO

WYOMING

SOUTH DAKOTA

NEVADA

NEBRASKA

CALIFORNIA

COLORADO

UTAH

KANSAS

ARIZONA

NEW MEXICO

OKLA

TEXAS

ALASKA

HAWAII

NEW HAMPSHIRE

VERMONT

MAINE

NNESOTA

WISCONSIN

MASSACHUSETTS

NEW YORK

RHODE ISLAND

CONNECTICUT

MICHIGAN

IOWA

INDIANA

OHIO

PENNSYLVANIA

NEW JERSEY

DELAWARE

ILLINOIS

MARYLAND

WEST VIRGINIA

VIRGINIA

MISSOURI

KENTUCKY

NORTH CAROLINA

TENNESSEE

ARKANSAS

SOUTH CAROLINA

MISSISSIPPI

GEORGIA

ALABAMA

FLORIDA

LOUISIANA

Alabama

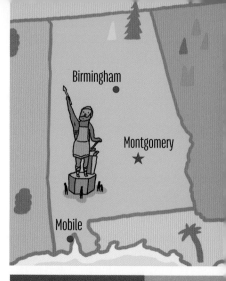

Cherokee, Creek, Choctaw, and Chickasaw Indians lived in Alabama thousands of years before Spanish explorers, searching for gold, arrived in the mid-1500s. More than 140 years later, the French built the first permanent European settlement, Mobile, in 1702.

Most of the region changed hands—among the French, English, and Americans—several times during the next hundred years. After capturing Mobile during the War of 1812, the U.S. controlled all of present-day Alabama. It became a state in 1819.

Cotton plantations dominated Alabama in the early 1800s. As a slave state, Alabama withdrew from the Union in 1861, at the start of the Civil War. The first capital of the Confederacy—the government formed by states that had broken away from the Union—was located in Montgomery. Seven years later, Alabama was readmitted to the United States.

Cotton remained an important commodity after the war. Deposits of coal and iron helped the state to establish a steel industry. By the end of the 1800s, Alabama was highly industrialized. In the 1950s and 1960s, racial segregation led to conflicts that contributed to the American civil rights movement. Martin Luther King, Jr., gained national attention in Alabama in 1955 during a successful boycott to end discrimination on Montgomery buses.

Today, the paper and chemical industries are important sources of jobs for Alabama residents. Birmingham, the most populous city, is a leader in medical research.

The 22nd State

Admitted to Union: December 14, 1819

Postal Abbreviation: AL

Capital: Montgomery

Nickname: Heart of Dixie

Population: 4,859,000

Land Area: 50,645 square miles (131,171 sq. km)

State Tree: Longleaf pine

State Bird: Yellowhammer

The arrest of Rosa Parks sparked the Montgomery bus boycott. A year later, buses were integrated.

Alaska

Alaska's native peoples—including the Athabascans, Yup'iks, Tlingit, Inupiat, and Aleuts—arrived from Asia between 12,000 and 18,000 years ago. They lived in this vast land by themselves until 1784, when the Russians established a settlement on Kodiak Island. The Russians began setting up fur-trading posts, mining for coal, fishing, and hunting whales. No more than 900 Russian settlers ever lived in the territory at any one time. By the 1860s, Russia was eager to sell the land. The U.S. bought it in 1867 for $7 million—about two cents an acre.

The population of the territory grew slowly until the discovery of gold there in 1896. Thousands of miners traveled to this remote region to strike it rich. It became the 49th state in 1959. In 1968, the largest oil field in North America was found at Prudhoe Bay in the Arctic.

Alaska is still a wide-open frontier with a little more than one person per square mile. Barrow, Alaska, is the northernmost town in America. The sun never sets there between May 10 and August 2, and never rises between November 18 and January 23. Jobs and revenue come mostly from oil and gas, fishing, timber, and tourism. Juneau, the capital city, is located in the world's northernmost rain forest. Just miles from the city, visitors can see glaciers, hike mountains, and relax at the beach. The challenge for Alaskans today is to use the state's valuable resources while protecting its unique wilderness.

Traditionally, native Alaskans carve totem poles from single tree trunks.

The 49th State

Admitted to Union: January 3, 1959

Postal Abbreviation: AK

Capital: Juneau

Nickname: Last Frontier

Population: 738,400

Land Area: 570,641 square miles (1,477,953 sq. km)

State Tree: Sitka spruce

State Bird: Willow ptarmigan

Arizona

Flagstaff

Phoenix ★ Mesa

Tucson

Hohokam Indians built canals to water the Arizona desert more than 1,000 years before the first Spanish explorers arrived. Marcos de Niza passed through in 1539. Francisco Vásquez de Coronado followed in 1540, looking for cities of gold.

The Spanish set up Catholic missions in the 1600s and early 1700s. Spain founded its first settlement at Tubac in 1752.

In the early 1800s, Arizona was part of Mexico, which became independent from Spain in 1821. It remained a thinly populated region on Mexico's northern frontier until the U.S. gained control of the area in 1848 after winning the Mexican-American War.

That all changed with the discovery of gold, silver, and copper in the late 1800s, which attracted more settlers. Railroads were built across the region to bring them in. Arizona became a state in 1912, but its growth was limited by its heat and dryness.

The U.S. government helped to bring water to the desert. Dams—including the huge Hoover Dam, which was completed in 1936—created electricity and helped to water farms. Cotton became an important crop.

Arizona's population boomed during and after World War II, following the construction of military bases throughout the state, and centered mostly on Phoenix and its new manufacturing industry. By the 1960s, the widespread use of air-conditioning made desert living more comfortable. Today, Arizona is one of the nation's fastest-growing states.

The 48th State

Admitted to Union: February 14, 1912

Postal Abbreviation: AZ

Capital: Phoenix

Nickname: Grand Canyon State

Population: 6,828,000

Land Area: 113,594 square miles (294,207 sq. km)

State Tree: Blue paloverde

State Bird: Cactus wren

Grand Canyon National Park

Arkansas

Ancient Indian tribes settled in Arkansas about 12,000 years ago. But the recorded history of the state begins in 1541, when tribes such as the Quapaw, Caddo, Chickasaw, and Osage lived there. That year, Spanish explorer Hernando de Soto passed through the area in search of riches. (He did not find any.) The French explorer René-Robert Cavelier, sieur de La Salle claimed the region for France in 1682, as part of what he called Louisiana. Four years later, Italian explorer Henri de Tonti founded the first European settlement in Arkansas.

The U.S. gained Arkansas in 1803 as part of the Louisiana Purchase. In the 1820s and 1830s, the federal government forced Indians off the land, and white farmers moved in. Arkansas was admitted to the Union as a slave state in 1836. During the Civil War, Arkansas joined the Confederacy, the government formed in 1861 by southern states that had seceded—broken away—from the Union.

Cotton plantations thrived in the rich lowlands of the Mississippi and Arkansas Rivers. But in the early 1900s, rice replaced cotton as Arkansas's most important crop. The state went through hard economic times in the early years of the 20th century. Jobs were scarce, and many of Arkansas's farmers had to leave the state in search of work.

Since then, Arkansas's economy has improved, with food processing and lumber production taking their place alongside agriculture. And the state's natural beauty has spurred the growth of a new industry—tourism.

Mount Magazine State Park, Ozark Mountains

The 25th State

Admitted to Union: June 15, 1836

Postal Abbreviation: AR

Capital: Little Rock

Nickname: Natural State

Population: 2,978,200

Land Area: 52,035 square miles (134,771 sq. km)

State Tree: Loblolly pine

State Bird: Northern mockingbird

California

When Spanish explorer Juan Rodríguez Cabrillo traveled the California coast in 1542, the area was home to Cahuilla Indians. Still, he claimed the land for Spain. It remained an isolated frontier until 1769, when the Spanish began to set up forts and missions.

After Mexico gained its independence from Spain in 1821, California became a Mexican province. Once word spread of California's fertile soil and mild climate, Americans began heading west in growing numbers. But California did not become an American territory until the end of the Mexican-American War in 1848.

The discovery of gold at Sutter's Mill, north of San Francisco, in 1848 drew hundreds of thousands of newcomers during the California Gold Rush. After statehood was achieved in 1850, California's population continued to expand. The Pony Express, the telegraph, and the First Transcontinental Railroad linked California with the rest of the nation by the 1860s.

The early 1900s saw the growth of a new industry: moviemaking. Manufacturing and agriculture also grew. Irrigation pipelines brought water from the wet northern part of the state to the fast-growing, drier southern part.

Today, California has the nation's largest population, and Silicon Valley, in Northern California, is home to most of the country's growing technology and Internet industry. Balancing growth with preservation of the land is a constant challenge.

Big Sur's rugged coastline stretches 85 miles.

The 31st State

Admitted to Union: September 9, 1850

Abbreviation: CA

Capital: Sacramento

Nickname: Golden State

Population: 39,145,000

Land Area: 155,779 square miles (403,466 sq. km)

State Trees: Coast redwood, giant sequoia

State Bird: California quail

Colorado

Arapaho, Cheyenne, Apache, and Comanche Indians roamed Eastern Colorado long before Spanish explorers arrived in the 1600s. Both the Spanish and French claimed the area. In 1803, the U.S. bought what is today Eastern Colorado as part of the Louisiana Purchase from France.

The mountainous west was still controlled by Spain. It became part of Mexico in 1821. But after losing the Mexican-American War in 1848, Mexico was forced to give it to the U.S.

Large groups of settlers reached Colorado in the late 1850s, when gold was discovered in Pikes Peak Country, near present-day Denver. Growth driven by mining helped Colorado become a state in 1876. Soon after, a silver-mining boom brought even more people.

Water has also been important to Colorado's growth. Its dry eastern plains needed irrigation to become rich farmland. Farm production increased in the late 1800s, with sugar beets as the main crop. By the early 1900s, farming surpassed mining as the state's main industry. Since then, the government has built dams and pipelines to bring in water.

The Rocky Mountains loom large in Colorado. Its capital, Denver, is known as the Mile High City because it is exactly one mile (5,280 feet) above sea level. The state produces coal, oil, and gas; and farms millet, sorghum, and sheep. In recent years, tourism has become important. Aspen and Vail are popular ski resorts. Beautiful scenery and resource wealth continue to help Colorado grow at a rapid pace.

The 38th State

Admitted to Union: August 1, 1876

Postal Abbreviation: CO

Capital: Denver

Nickname: Centennial State

Population: 5,456,600

Land Area: 103,642 square miles (268,431 sq. km)

State Tree: Colorado blue spruce

State Bird: Lark bunting

Skiing is a big part of Colorado's tourism industry, which drew more than 70 million visitors to the state in 2015.

Connecticut

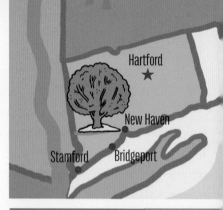

Algonquian Indian groups called Connecticut home long before Europeans arrived. In 1633, the Dutch built a small fort where Hartford now stands.

But Connecticut's first permanent European settlers migrated from the Massachusetts Bay Colony in search of religious freedom. They established villages in the Connecticut River Valley and near the Long Island Sound in 1636. Two other colonies, Saybrook and New Haven, eventually became part of the Connecticut Colony. By 1654, the English settlers had forced the Dutch out.

Most Connecticut colonists supported independence from Britain. During the American Revolution (1775–1783), the colony supplied food and gunpowder to George Washington's army. In 1788, Connecticut became the fifth state of the new nation.

Farming was important here until the late 1800s. But local inventors helped industry grow as well. Eli Whitney, famous for his cotton gin, also made parts for guns. Eli Terry was the first person to mass-produce clocks. Bicycles, pins, and textiles were also made in the state. After the Civil War (1861–1865), European immigrants came to the state for work.

Today, Connecticut produces hardware, aircraft parts, and submarines. Some of the country's largest insurance companies and bioscience researchers are based here, too. Connecticut's small villages and old country lanes, which recall historical New England, make it a popular place to vacation.

The 5th State

Admitted to Union: January 9, 1788

Postal Abbreviation: CT

Capital: Hartford

Nickname: Constitution State

Population: 3,591,000

Land Area: 4,842 square miles (12,542 sq. km)

State Tree: White oak

State Bird: American robin

The Mystic Seaport area was once a major shipbuilding center.

Delaware

Delaware was a battleground in its early years, changing hands several times. Henry Hudson, a British explorer sailing for the Dutch, was the first European to see its coast, in 1609. At the time, Nanticoke, Susquehanna, and Lenni-Lenape (also called Delaware) Indians inhabited the area.

In 1631, the Dutch built their first colony at what is now called Lewes. However, Nanticoke Indians burned it to the ground after a dispute with the settlers. Swedish colonists established Fort Christina, now Wilmington, along the coast in 1638, but the Dutch soon chased them away. In 1664, the English captured the Dutch colonies of New Netherland (New York) and the Delaware settlements.

During the American Revolution (1775–1783), British troops occupied Wilmington for a few weeks. But no major battles took place there. In 1787, Delaware ratified the U.S. Constitution and became the first state of the new nation. Though a slave state, it remained in the Union during the Civil War (1861–1865).

Delaware is a state of north-south contrast. Starting in the 1800s, chemical, shipbuilding, and other manufacturing plants were built around Wilmington in the north. Today, banking, insurance, and real estate companies are based there. The state's business-friendly laws encourage all kinds of companies to set up shop. But Southern Delaware is more dependent on agriculture. Poultry, soybean, wheat, and corn farms dot the rolling coastal plain.

The city of New Castle was founded in 1640.

The 1st State

Admitted to Union: December 7, 1787

Postal Abbreviation: DE

Capital: Dover

Nickname: First State

Population: 946,000

Land Area: 1,949 square miles (5,047 sq. km)

State Tree: American holly

State Bird: Delaware blue hen

Florida

Spanish explorer Juan Ponce de León led an expedition to Florida in 1513, searching for the mythical Fountain of Youth. He didn't find it, but he claimed the land for Spain. St. Augustine was founded in 1565. For more than 200 years, the Spanish, French, and British sought control of Florida, until Spain traded it to Great Britain for Havana, Cuba, in 1763. Spain regained control of some of Florida after the American Revolution, but the U.S. won it back in the Adams-Onis Treaty, which took effect in 1821. At the time, Seminole Indians held some of the area's best land. To make room for European settlers, the U.S. government bought most of their land and forced those who would not sell to move west to Indian Territory (now Oklahoma). In 1845, Florida was admitted to the Union as a slave state. It joined the Confederacy at the start of the Civil War and rejoined the Union in 1868.

Florida developed quickly after the war. Businessmen Henry Flagler and Henry Plant built railroad tracks that opened up land as far south as Miami. Swamps, including the Everglades, were drained. Farmers planted citrus trees. Resort cities grew along the coast. Tourists and new residents poured into the state.

In recent decades, South Florida has become home to many Latin Americans and people from the Caribbean. Tourism is important to Florida's economy—each year, about 100 million tourists travel there to visit its beaches and resorts. Agriculture is important, too—the state grows about 70 percent of the country's citrus fruit.

The 27th State

Admitted to Union: March 3, 1845

Postal Abbreviation: FL

Capital: Tallahassee

Nickname: Sunshine State

Population: 20,271,300

Land Area: 53,625 square miles (138,887 sq. km)

State Tree: Sabal palm

State Bird: Northern mockingbird

Florida's Kennedy Space Center at Cape Canaveral was home to the U.S. space shuttle program until 2011. Today, it serves as a launch site for government and commercial rockets.

Georgia

When Spanish explorer Hernando de Soto arrived here in about 1540, he found Creek and Cherokee Indians in large villages, where they farmed corn, beans, and squash. Starting in the 1560s, the Spanish built settlements along the coast.

In 1732, King George II gave a group of Englishmen permission to start the Georgia colony. James Oglethorpe, the group's leader, wanted it to be a place where poor English people could start a new life. He led the first 120 settlers to present-day Savannah in 1733. Oglethorpe limited the size of farms and would not permit slavery. Eventually, both of these rules changed, after the king took direct control of Georgia in 1752.

In 1788, Georgia became the fourth state. Cotton farming expanded—partly on land that Indians had occupied. The Creek sold their land and moved west, but some Cherokee resisted. By 1837, U.S. troops had forced some 15,000 Creek to move to Indian Territory (now Oklahoma). Thousands died along the "Trail of Tears."

Georgia joined the Confederacy in the Civil War. In 1864, Union general William T. Sherman led battle troops through Georgia, from Atlanta to Savannah, destroying farms, factories, and rail lines.

Georgia grows more pecans and peanuts than any other state. Nut and cotton farms exist alongside textile factories and chemical plants. Television production and broadcasting are centered in Atlanta, Georgia's largest city.

Historic homes are open to visitors in Savannah.

The 4th State

Admitted to Union: January 2, 1788

Postal Abbreviation: GA

Capital: Atlanta

Nickname: Peach State

Population: 10,214,300

Land Area: 57,513 square miles (148,959 sq. km)

State Tree: Southern live oak

State Birds: Brown thrasher and northern bobwhite quail

Hawaii

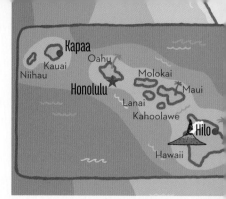

Polynesian people reached the Hawaiian Islands about 2,000 years ago. British explorer James Cook arrived in 1778—the first European to set foot on Hawaii. Other explorers and traders soon followed. Eventually, Hawaii became a water and supply stop for ships crossing the Pacific. American whaling and trading ships began to dock here in the early 1800s. Missionaries came in 1820.

Large-scale farming on the islands' rich volcanic soil began in 1835, when Americans started the first sugar plantation. With a shortage of local labor, people were brought in from China, Japan, Portugal, and the Philippines to work the fields.

By the middle of the 19th century, the native Hawaiian population was dwindling. Newcomers carried diseases for which the islanders had no immunity. Many died. There were about 300,000 native Hawaiians when Cook arrived. By 1853, only about 70,000 remained.

In the late 1800s, American farm and business owners were very powerful. They helped to force Queen Liliuokalani from power in 1893. The following year, Hawaii was declared a republic. Hawaii became a U.S. territory in 1898. After decades of work by local leaders, Hawaii became a state in 1959, making it the last to join the Union.

Agriculture remains important in Hawaii. But spectacular beaches, volcanic mountains, and lush forests have made tourism key to the state's economy.

Ka'ena Point State Park in Oahu

The 50th State

Admitted to Union: August 21, 1959

Postal Abbreviation: HI

Capital: Honolulu

Nickname: Aloha State

Population: 1,431,600

Land Area: 6,423 square miles (16,635 sq. km)

State Tree: Kukui (candlenut tree)

State Bird: Nene (Hawaiian goose)

Idaho

The first white settlers to see Idaho were members of the Lewis and Clark expedition, who were sent west by President Thomas Jefferson to explore after the Louisiana Purchase in 1803. In the years that followed, a few trading posts were established, but the U.S. and Great Britain each claimed the area. The U.S. acquired Idaho from Great Britain as part of Oregon Country in the Oregon Treaty of 1846. When gold was discovered in the 1860s, a wave of miners and settlers followed.

This new settlement sparked conflicts with local Indian tribes such as the Nez Percé and the Bannock, who were being pushed off their land. Some tribes staged violent rebellions, and many were forced to live on reservations. Railroads entered the region in the 1880s and 1890s, paving the way for more white settlers to set out for Idaho. After Idaho became a state in 1890, the federal government built dams and canals that brought water from the Snake River to Idaho's rich but dry soils. Farm acreage increased. After World War II, the manufacturing and food-processing industries also grew, and people from rural areas moved to cities, such as Boise, for jobs.

In 1951, electricity was generated from nuclear power for the first time at the National Reactor Testing Station near Idaho Falls. In recent decades, Boise has become the headquarters for several large computer, timber, and food-processing companies. As the state grows, its rich soil, abundant forests, and minerals continue to be important for its future.

Coeur d'Alene

Boise

Idaho Falls

Pocatello

The 43rd State

Admitted to Union: July 3, 1890

Postal Abbreviation: ID

Capital: Boise

Nickname: Gem State

Population: 1,655,000

Land Area: 82,643 square miles (214,045 sq. km)

State Tree: Western white pine

State Bird: Mountain bluebird

Tourists enjoy rafting on the Salmon River.

Illinois

Rockford

Chicago

Peoria

★
Springfield

Thousands of years ago, the first people of Illinois built huge burial mounds that still dot the state. When French explorers Jacques Marquette and Louis Jolliet arrived in 1673, Cahokia and Ojibwa Indians populated the region.

The French set up fur-trading posts and small settlements in the late 1600s and early 1700s. But the area's population did not really begin to grow until after the American Revolution (1775–1783). When Illinois became a state in 1818, it did not technically have enough people for statehood. Congress made an exception because of the area's rich farmland and the country's desire for westward expansion. The opening of the Erie Canal in 1825 created a water route from the Atlantic Ocean to the Great Lakes. European immigrants and settlers from the Eastern U.S. poured into Northern Illinois, eager for work.

Illinois stayed in the Union during the Civil War (1861–1865), but many people in Southern Illinois sympathized with the South. After the war, industry boomed. Chicago became the nation's meatpacking and grain center. And when a fire started in a small barn in October 1871, destroying an area 4 miles wide and 1 mile long within 24 hours, the city was quickly rebuilt and modernized.

Today, Northern Illinois is largely urban and industrial. Chicago, its hub, is a center for iron and steel production and other manufacturing. Southern Illinois has many farms, and corn remains an important crop.

The 21st State

Admitted to Union: December 3, 1818

Postal Abbreviation: IL

Capital: Springfield

Nickname: Land of Lincoln, the Prairie State

Population: 12,860,000

Land Area: 55,519 square miles (143,793 sq. km)

State Tree: White oak

State Bird: Northern cardinal

The Willis Tower, commonly referred to as the Sears Tower, is the second-tallest building in the United States.

Indiana

When French explorer René-Robert Cavelier, sieur de La Salle came through Indiana in 1679, Miami and Potawatomi Indians inhabited the region. More than 30 years later, in 1717, Indiana's first European settlement was established at Ouiatenon, near what is now West Lafayette. Vincennes, established in 1732, was the first lasting settlement.

Beaver hats were popular in Europe, so the animal's fur became valuable. French and British businessmen competed to control the region's fur trade in the 1700s. After the French and Indian War in 1763, the British gained all French-held land east of the Mississippi, including Indiana. But they lost it after the American Revolution (1775–1783). In 1783, Indiana became part of the Northwest Territory.

Conflict continued as Indians, including famed Ottawa war leader Pontiac, resisted white settlement. But American victories at Fallen Timbers (1794) and Tippecanoe (1811) pushed Indians off the land. Settlers streamed in to take advantage of the area's rich farmland. In 1816, Indiana became a state.

In the late 1800s, Indiana's industries expanded. Natural gas was discovered, and the Standard Oil Company built a huge refinery in the state. In 1906, U.S. Steel constructed its biggest plant in the northwestern corner of the state, and the city of Gary was built up around it.

Agriculture is also important. Indiana farmers grow corn, wheat, and soybeans. The state is also a top poultry producer.

The Indianapolis 500 is held at the Indianapolis Motor Speedway in Speedway, Indiana.

The 19th State

Admitted to Union: December 11, 1816

Postal Abbreviation: IN

Capital: Indianapolis

Nickname: Hoosier State

Population: 6,619,700

Land Area: 35,826 square miles (92,789 sq. km)

State Tree: Tulip poplar

State Bird: Northern cardinal

Iowa

Sioux City

Cedar Rapids

Davenport

★ Des Moines

Prehistoric Indians, called mound builders, were Iowa's first inhabitants. By the time French explorers Jacques Marquette and Louis Jolliet arrived in 1673, tribes such as the Illinois, Miami, Sioux, and Omaha had replaced the earliest people.

Once part of French Louisiana, Iowa became U.S. land in 1803 when Thomas Jefferson bought the territory from France, as part of the Louisiana Purchase. During the first few decades after the Purchase, the region was not open to white settlement. But by the 1830s, settlers in Illinois were pushing the Sauk and Fox Indians west. So a strip of land in Iowa was set aside for them along the west bank of the Mississippi River. The Black Hawk War broke out when the Indians refused to move to this set-aside region.

An 1833 treaty with the U.S. government opened the Indian lands to white settlers. People poured in, eager to take advantage of Iowa's rich farmland. In 1846, Iowa became a state. And by 1851, all Indian lands had been given to the U.S. government.

Iowa's eastern border is defined by the Mississippi River, and its western border is the Missouri River. It has some of the most fertile soil in the world. Farms cover about 90 percent of the state. Although there are fewer farms than in past decades, agriculture and businesses connected with farming—including manufacturing, which is now the largest sector of the state's economy—employ the greatest number of Iowa residents.

The 29th State

Admitted to Union: December 28, 1846

Postal Abbreviation: IA

Capital: Des Moines

Nickname: Hawkeye State

Population: 3,124,000

Land Area: 55,857 square miles (144,669 sq. km)

State Tree: Bur oak

State Bird: Eastern goldfinch

An attendee of the Iowa State Fair rests with Ida, a Brown Swiss cow from his family farm.

Kansas

The recorded history of Kansas began when Spanish explorer Francisco Vásquez de Coronado crossed its grassy plains in 1541. Pawnee and Kansa (now Kaw) Indians inhabited the region. With the 1803 Louisiana Purchase, Kansas became a U.S. territory.

Starting in the 1830s, the government used Kansas to temporarily settle Indians whom it had pushed off their native lands farther east. In 1854, the Kansas-Nebraska Act opened those territories to whites. When several Southern states left the Union in 1861, at the start of the Civil War, anti-slavery members of Congress finally had the power to make Kansas a slave-free state.

Between 1866 and 1885, cowboys drove herds of cattle from Texas to Kansas railroad towns such as Dodge City, Abilene, and Wichita. The cattle were then moved east on the trains. But the cowboys—weary from the trail and looking for fun—often hung around, getting into trouble. Lawmen such as Wyatt Earp, "Bat" Masterson, and "Wild Bill" Hickok are famous for establishing order.

Buffalo still roam free at the Tallgrass Prairie National Preserve in Eastern Kansas, but much of the Kansas plains now grow wheat, corn, and soy instead of wild grasses. In Wichita, factories produce airplanes. There are still cowboys working in the beef industry in Kansas, but they drive trucks as often as they ride horses in the wide-open spaces that are still an important part of the state's character. Kansas also produces oil.

Schoolhouse in the Tallgrass Prairie National Preserve in Eastern Kansas

The 34th State

Admitted to Union: January 29, 1861

Postal Abbreviation: KS

Capital: Topeka

Nickname: Sunflower State

Population: 2,911,600

Land Area: 81,759 square miles (211,754 sq. km)

State Tree: Eastern cottonwood

State Bird: Western meadowlark

Kentucky

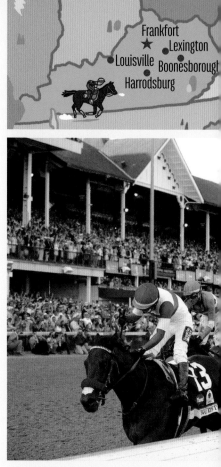

Explorers Thomas Walker and Christopher Gist wandered across Kentucky in the early 1750s. British law did not allow colonists to settle west of the Appalachian Mountains, and local Indians, such as the Shawnee and the Iroquois, resisted the newcomers. Still, Harrodsburg was established in 1774. A year later, explorer Daniel Boone led pioneers across the Cumberland Gap to found Boonesborough.

Frequent battles between settlers and Indians took place during the American Revolution (1775–1783). After the war, settlers made their way to the fertile Bluegrass region. Louisville was founded alongside the Ohio River in 1778. Originally part of Virginia, Kentucky became a state in 1792.

Kentucky was divided on the issue of slavery. During the Civil War (1861–1865), it supplied troops to both the free Union states and the slaveholding states of the Confederacy. When the Confederate army entered the state in 1861, however, Kentucky became a part of the Union.

Eastern Kentucky was the last part of the state to be settled. When railroads arrived in the 1860s, it became easier to harvest important resources such as lumber and coal.

Kentucky has been a center for horse breeding since the mid-1700s. Today, the state has world-class horse farms. Coal has remained important, but the state's economy also depends on tobacco, manufacturing (especially of automobiles), and tourism.

Churchill Downs Racetrack, in Louisville, KY, is the site of the Kentucky Derby, the oldest continuously running sports event in the nation.

The 15th State

Admitted to Union: June 1, 1792

Postal Abbreviation: KY

Capital: Frankfort

Nickname: Bluegrass State

Population: 4,425,100

Land Area: 39,486 square miles (102,269 sq. km)

State Tree: Tulip poplar

State Bird: Northern cardinal

Louisiana

Several Indian nations, including the Tunica and Caddo, were among Louisiana's first occupants. Spanish explorer Hernando de Soto crossed the area in 1542. But when he didn't find gold, he moved on. Then, in 1682, René-Robert Cavelier, sieur de la Salle claimed all the land from the Mississippi River to the Rocky Mountains for France. The area was called French Louisiana.

At the end of the French and Indian War in 1763, France had to give the territory to Spain. But in 1802, Spain secretly transferred it back to France. President Thomas Jefferson did not want this powerful European nation to control land that was so close to the U.S. So in 1803, he sent James Monroe to France to negotiate for the parts of the territory east of the Mississippi River, only to be offered the entire Louisiana Territory. The Louisiana Purchase doubled the size of the young country. The U.S. would eventually carve all or part of 15 states from the territory. In 1812, land in the southern region became the state of Louisiana.

Today, Louisiana has one of the South's most diverse populations. The city of New Orleans has strong French, Spanish, American Indian, and African roots. Its warm climate, lively music, unique foods, and festivals attract tourists from around the world. However, because of its low elevation, the city will face challenges as a result of rising sea levels caused by global climate change.

Oil, gas, and chemical industries are important to the state's economy.

The 18th State

Admitted to Union: April 30, 1812

Postal Abbreviation: LA

Capital: Baton Rouge

Nickname: Pelican State

Population: 4,670,700

Land Area: 43,204 square miles (111,898 sq. km)

State Tree: Bald cypress

State Bird: Brown pelican

A big celebration called Mardi Gras takes place in New Orleans each year.

Maine

Algonquian-speaking Abenaki Indian tribes lived in Maine for thousands of years before the first European ships reached its rocky coast in the 1500s. In the 1620s, English settlers established villages along Maine's sheltered coves and on its tiny islands. These isolated settlements joined the growing Massachusetts Bay Colony in the 1650s. To encourage settlement in its northern province, colonial leaders offered free land to people willing to live in Maine. Many accepted, and the region grew quickly in the mid-1700s.

During the American Revolution (1775–1783), British ships attacked Maine's coastal towns. Falmouth (today's Portland) was burned. Since the Massachusetts government couldn't protect Maine, some Mainers decided it was time to control their own affairs. Maine was separated from Massachusetts after the War of 1812.

Competition for power between free and slave states in the early 1800s influenced Maine's history. Under the Missouri Compromise, Maine entered the Union as a free state in 1820. A year later, Missouri was admitted as a slave state.

In the early 1900s, Maine's rushing rivers powered textile mills and shoe manufacturing plants. Today, Maine's extensive forests provide paper and wood products, and farmers grow potatoes and apples and harvest blueberries and maple syrup. Fishing and shipping have long been important to Maine's economy, and the state is perhaps most famous for its lobsters.

The 23rd State

Admitted to Union: March 15, 1820

Postal Abbreviation: ME

Capital: Augusta

Nickname: Pine Tree State

Population: 1,329,300

Land Area: 30,843 square miles (79,883 sq. km)

State Tree: Eastern white pine

State Bird: Black-capped chickadee

Acadia was the first national park east of the Mississippi River.

Maryland

Nanticoke and Piscataway Indians were living in Maryland when Europeans learned of the area. In 1632, King Charles I of England granted the lands of Maryland to Cecilius Calvert, 2nd Lord Baltimore. Colonists arrived from England two years later. They established the first permanent settlements at St. Mary's City. Calvert, who was Catholic, saw Maryland as a place where people could enjoy religious freedom, and in 1649, Maryland's leaders passed a law that granted freedom of religion to all Christians.

In 1788, Maryland became the seventh state when it approved the U.S. Constitution. It escaped most of the fighting during the American Revolution. But many battles occurred there during the War of 1812. On September 12, 1814, Francis Scott Key wrote the lyrics to "The Star-Spangled Banner" as he watched a British ship bombard Baltimore's Fort McHenry.

During the Civil War, Marylanders were divided. The Mason-Dixon line, which runs through the state, marked the division between north and south. Although it was a slave state, Maryland remained in the Union. Still, many Marylanders fought for the Confederacy.

Maryland's industries expanded in the early 20th century, led by electronics, food products, and chemical manufacturing. Most industries are concentrated around Baltimore and near Washington, D.C. Chesapeake Bay—with its fishing, boating, and scenic shoreline—is an important area for business and visitors.

Main Street in Annapolis has brick roads and colonial-style buildings.

The 7th State

Admitted to Union: April 28, 1788

Postal Abbreviation: MD

Capital: Annapolis

Nickname: Free State

Population: 6,006,400

Land Area: 9,707 square miles (25,142 sq. km)

State Tree: White oak

State Bird: Baltimore oriole

Massachusetts

Although Algonquian Indians have lived in Massachusetts for more than 10,000 years, the state's written history began in the early 1600s, when French and English ships explored and mapped the coast.

English Pilgrims seeking religious freedom established the first permanent settlement at Plymouth, in 1620. The Massachusetts Bay Colony followed in 1630. But colonial leaders allowed only the practice of their own religions, so several groups left to start new colonies in present-day Connecticut, Rhode Island, New Hampshire, and Maine.

In 1691, the Plymouth and Massachusetts Bay Colonies joined to form the Province of Massachusetts. It became a center for rebellion in the years before the American Revolution. Led by Samuel Adams, Paul Revere, and the Sons of Liberty, colonists staged the 1773 Boston Tea Party to protest British taxes. Minutemen fired the first shots of the revolution at Lexington and Concord in April 1775. After the war, Massachusetts became the sixth state when it approved the U.S. Constitution in 1788.

Massachusetts's textile and shoe industries grew in the 1800s. The state also became a center for whaling and fishing.

Today, industry, education, and the arts thrive in Massachusetts. Boston is home to leading universities and medical centers, making it an important player in tech development and medical research. But fishing still remains a major industry as well. Its rich colonial history has made Massachusetts a favorite tourist destination.

The Boston Tea Party Ships and Museum in Fort Point Channel in Boston

The 6th State

Admitted to Union: February 6, 1788

Postal Abbreviation: MA

Capital: Boston

Nickname: Bay State

Population: 6,794,400

Land Area: 7,800 square miles (20,202 sq. km)

State Tree: American elm

State Bird: Black-capped chickadee or wild turkey

Michigan

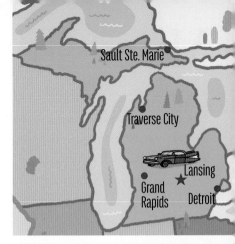

Potawatomi and Ojibwa Indians were living in Michigan's Upper Peninsula when French explorer Etienne Brûlé arrived in the early 1600s. Other explorers, missionaries, and fur trappers followed. Jacques Marquette established Michigan's first permanent European settlement, at Sault Ste. Marie in 1668. By the 1700s, there were several French missions, forts, and farms in the region.

The British gained control of Michigan in 1763, after the French and Indian War. After the American Revolution, the U.S. took over most of the land. It became part of the Northwest Territory in 1787. The U.S. reclaimed Detroit and the Upper Peninsula during the War of 1812, and Michigan became a state in 1837. Iron mines opened after statehood. With the completion of the Soo Locks in 1855, barges began to transport iron ore to steel manufacturing plants on the Great Lakes. In the late 1800s, the lumber and furniture industries grew to take advantage of Michigan's forests.

By the early 20th century, industrialists had begun automobile production in Detroit, located in Michigan's Lower Peninsula. It's still an important industry. Today, most of the state's people live in the Lower Peninsula. Its farms produce apples, grapes, cherries, sugar beets, and other crops. Michigan's remote Upper Peninsula depends on mining, logging, and tourism. Much of it has remained unchanged since the first explorers and trappers passed through the region centuries ago.

The 26th State

Admitted to Union: January 26, 1837

Postal Abbreviation: MI

Capital: Lansing

Nickname: Wolverine State, Great Lake State

Population: 9,922,600

Land Area: 56,539 square miles (146,435 sq. km)

State Tree: Eastern white pine

State Bird: American robin

The Big Sable Point Lighthouse is located on Lake Michigan.

Minnesota

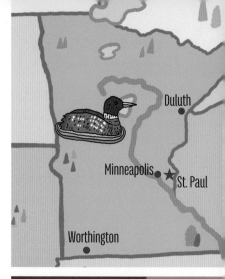

Ojibwa and Sioux Indians lived in Minnesota when French explorers, fur traders, and missionaries, including Jacques Marquette, Pierre Esprit Radisson, and Médard des Groseilliers, arrived in the late 1600s. Still, France claimed the area as part of French Louisiana.

President Jefferson bought the land from France in 1803 as part of the Louisiana Purchase. The region was remote, but settlers from New England and Canada trickled in to plant crops and log the forests.

Minnesota became a U.S. territory in 1849. At the time, there were few people in the area. When the U.S. government forced Indians to give up land in Southern Minnesota, however, farmers came to work the thick prairie soil.

In 1858, Minnesota became a state. Eager to increase the population, the Minnesota government advertised in Northern Europe for settlers. In 1862, the U.S. Congress passed the Homestead Act, which promised free land to settlers. Soon, people from Norway, Sweden, Germany, and Denmark began to arrive. Many of today's Minnesotans are descendants of these immigrants.

Mining for iron ore and manufacturing continue to be important to the state's economy. Industries such as electronics and food processing, services such as banking and insurance, and farming for crops including sugar beets, corn, and green peas employ many people. Tourists are drawn to the state's sparkling lakes and deep forests.

The 32nd State

Admitted to Union: May 11, 1858

Postal Abbreviation: MN

Capital: St. Paul

Nicknames: Gopher State, Land of 10,000 Lakes

Population: 5,489,600

Land Area: 79,627 square miles (128,147 sq. km)

State Tree: Red pine

State Bird: Common loon

The Mall of America, in Bloomington, Minnesota, is the largest shopping mall in the United States.

Mississippi

When Spanish explorer Hernando de Soto traveled through Mississippi in 1540, Choctaw, Chickasaw, and other Indian groups were living in the area. France claimed Mississippi as part of the Louisiana Territory in the late 1600s and established settlements at Ocean Spring (1699) and Natchez (1716). As part of the Treaty of Paris, which ended the French and Indian War in 1763, the land came under British control. But they turned it over to the U.S. after the American Revolution.

Mississippi became a state in 1817. During the 1830s, the U.S. government forced the remaining Indians out, sending them west to Indian Territory. Soon huge cotton plantations worked by slaves were built across the state.

Mississippi joined the Confederacy during the Civil War, and many battles were fought here. Union general Ulysses S. Grant won the decisive Battle of Vicksburg, giving the Union control of the Mississippi River.

Racial discrimination continued to be a problem after slavery ended. During the 1960s, violent clashes occurred as black citizens struggled for equal rights.

Throughout its history, the Mississippi River has been an important resource for the state. In the 1800s, steamboats carried passengers to cities along the river. Today, the rich soils of the Mississippi Delta support agriculture.

Cotton is still vital to the state's economy. But logging, fish harvesting, gambling, tourism, and manufacturing have become increasingly important.

The Mississippi river was named after an Indian word meaning "father of waters."

The 20th State

Admitted to Union: December 10, 1817

Postal Abbreviation: MS

Capital: Jackson

Nickname: Magnolia State

Population: 2,992,300

Land Area: 46,923 square miles (121,531 sq. km)

State Tree: Southern magnolia

State Bird: Northern mockingbird or wood duck

Missouri

The Osage, Missouri, and Fox Indians, among others, inhabited Missouri when French explorers—Jacques Marquette, Louis Jolliet, and René-Robert, sieur de La Salle—first traveled down the Mississippi River in the late 1600s. Missouri was part of the land La Salle claimed for France as the Louisiana Territory. The first permanent European settlement was established around 1735 at Ste. Genevieve. Several settlements followed, including St. Louis in 1764. Still, the area was never that important to France. When Napoléon Bonaparte needed money in 1803, he sold the entire Louisiana Territory to the U.S. Missouri was one of the regions gained in the Louisiana Purchase.

In 1821, Missouri entered the Union as a slave state—to balance the admission of Maine as a free state the year before. Soon Missouri became the gateway to the frontier, with the Oregon Trail starting in the city of Independence on its route to the west.

During the Civil War (1861–1865), Missouri was a border state—a slave state that remained in the Union. Bloody battles were fought there, with each side seeking control.

Farming is vitally important to present-day Missouri. Top crops include grain, hay, and soybeans, and mining for lead and limestone remains important. But the state's largest cities—St. Louis and Kansas City—are among the biggest transportation and industrial centers in the country, and St. Louis has a growing biotechnology industry.

The 24th State

Admitted to Union: August 10, 1821

Postal Abbreviation: MO

Capital: Jefferson City

Nickname: Show Me State

Population: 6,083,700

Land Area: 68,742 square miles (178,040 sq. km)

State Tree: Flowering dogwood

State Bird: Eastern bluebird

The St. Louis Gateway Arch bridges Missouri and Illinois.

Montana

Many Indian nations occupied Montana before European trappers crossed its plains and mountains in the early 1700s. But Montana's history as a part of the U.S. began in 1803, with the Louisiana Purchase. Hired by the federal government to survey the new territory, a team of explorers led by Meriwether Lewis and William Clark were the first Americans to see it.

A few fur traders and religious missionaries ventured to this remote land in the early 1800s. But large numbers of people didn't come until gold was discovered in 1852. Montana became a U.S. territory in 1864, mainly because of the need to bring law and order to the mining camps.

As settlers moved into Montana, conflicts between the U.S. Army and Indians became more frequent. In 1876, the Sioux and Cheyenne killed Army officer George Custer and more than 200 of his men in a famous battle near the Little Bighorn River. During the 1880s, railroads crossed Montana, and the territory became a state in 1889. Cattle and sheep ranchers looking for inexpensive land arrived throughout the early 1900s.

Today, the state's clean air, beautiful scenery, and wide-open spaces attract many visitors. More than 30 million acres—making up about a third of the land—are state or federal lands, including 16 million acres of national forest. Ski resorts, parks, and historical areas now allow people to use the state's resources in a way that also preserves them.

Glacier National Park has more than 700 miles of hiking trails.

The 41st State

Admitted to Union: November 8, 1889

Postal Abbreviation: MT

Capital: Helena

Nicknames: Treasure State, Big Sky Country

Population: 1,033,000

Land Area: 145,546 square miles (376,962 sq. km)

State Tree: Ponderosa pine

State Bird: Western meadowlark

39

Nebraska

Before white settlers arrived, several Indian groups lived in Nebraska—the Omaha, Pawnee, and Dakotas. Spain claimed the area in 1541. The French did the same in 1682. Neither nation created permanent settlements there. But in 1803, the Louisiana Purchase made the region part of the U.S.

The area's first permanent settlement, Bellevue, was established in 1822 along the Missouri River. Still, most of the people who entered Nebraska didn't stay. Pioneers passed through as they followed the Oregon Trail to the west. Some considered Nebraska's dry plains to be part of the "Great American Desert" and wrote that it was not fit for farming. Seeing little value in Nebraska, the federal government made it Indian Territory for the first half of the 1800s. White settlement was forbidden.

In 1854, the U.S. government changed its view. It forced Indians out and opened Nebraska to whites. The 1862 Homestead Act gave each settler 160 acres of land, as long as they lived on it for five years. New railroads brought even more people. In 1867, Nebraska became a state.

Farming expanded in Nebraska in the 1890s with irrigation. Now Nebraska contains some of the country's most productive farmland. Fields of corn and soybeans are common in the eastern part of the state, while wheat and cattle dominate the drier western counties. The city of Omaha is also home to many major corporations.

The 37th State
Admitted to Union: March 1, 1867

Postal Abbreviation: NE

Capital: Lincoln

Nickname: Cornhusker State

Population: 1,896,200

Land Area: 76,824 square miles (198,974 sq. km)

State Tree: Eastern cottonwood

State Bird: Western meadowlark

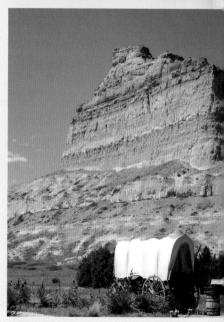

A wagon train reenactment on the Oregon Trail, Scotts Bluff National Monument, Nebraska

Nevada

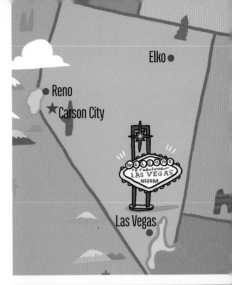

Until the mid-1800s, tribes including the Paiute, Shoshone, and Washoe had Nevada to themselves. European and American explorers and traders, such as Jedediah Smith, entered the region in the 1820s, looking for new sources of furs. Settlers passed through on their way to California during the 1830s and 1840s. But this dry and empty land was not a destination for most people. That changed in 1859 with the discovery of a huge silver deposit—the Comstock Lode. Prospectors poured in, making a boomtown of the nearby mining camp at Virginia City.

During the Civil War (1861–1865), President Abraham Lincoln pushed for Nevada statehood. He knew that many of Nevada's people were against slavery. Its voters would probably send anti-slavery senators to Congress, providing support for the Union cause. Although it didn't have the required population, Nevada became a state in 1864.

In 1936, construction was completed on a massive dam across the Colorado River at Lake Mead. Officially named in 1947, the Hoover Dam provides power for nearly 8 million people in Arizona, California, and Nevada. Today, mining is still important in Nevada. The state is a leader in production of gold, silver, and mercury. Cattle ranches and irrigated farms dot the plains and hills. But Nevada's biggest industry is tourism. Reno and Las Vegas attract visitors from around the world, and the beauty of Nevada's deserts and mountains draws thousands of nature lovers every year.

Nevada comes from a Spanish word meaning "snowcapped." It refers to the snowy peaks of the Sierra Nevada range near Carson City.

The 36th State

Admitted to Union: October 31, 1864

Postal Abbreviation: NV

Capital: Carson City

Nickname: Silver State

Population: 2,890,850

Land Area: 109,781 square miles (284,332 sq. km)

State Trees: Single-leaf pinyon, Great Basin bristlecone

State Bird: Mountain bluebird

41

New Hampshire

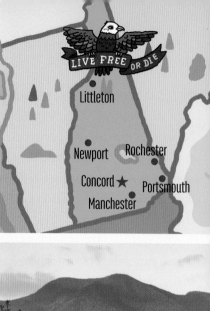

Algonquian Indians lived in New Hampshire before European explorers, including Samuel de Champlain, arrived in the early 1600s. Several small settlements, such as Odiorne Point (Rye), Strawbery Banke (Portsmouth), and Exeter, were already established along its bays and rivers by the end of the 1630s. In 1641, New Hampshire became part of the Massachusetts Bay Colony. It was made a separate colony 38 years later.

New Hampshire was a strong supporter of rebellion against England. In 1776, even before the U.S. Declaration of Independence was issued, the colony declared its own independence. Even though no battles were fought in the state, hundreds of New Hampshire men fought in the American Revolution (1775–1783). After the war, New Hampshire was the ninth state to join the Union.

During and after the Civil War (1861–1865), New Hampshire became increasingly industrial. Abundant water powered textile mills, and immigrants from Canada and Europe arrived to work in the state's factories.

During the two world wars, the Portsmouth Naval Shipyard built submarines. Factories made uniforms and shoes for soldiers. Today, the technology, tech manufacturing, and health-care industries provide jobs. So does the tourism industry. The White Mountain National Forest covers 800,000 acres. Its clear streams and rugged mountains make it a popular destination for vacationers.

Bright leaves bring color to the White Mountains in fall.

The 9th State

Admitted to Union: June 21, 1788

Postal Abbreviation: NH

Capital: Concord

Nickname: Granite State

Population: 1,330,600

Land Area: 8,953 square miles (23,187 sq. km)

State Tree: Paper birch

State Bird: Purple finch

New Jersey

New Jersey's recorded history began in 1524, when the Italian sailor Giovanni da Verrazzano explored its sandy shoreline. At the time, Lenape Indians lived in the area, hunting, fishing, and growing crops such as corn.

The Dutch placed their first settlement on the Hudson River in 1613. New Netherland was established a year later. In 1638, New Sweden was established on the Delaware River. The Dutch forced the Swedes out in 1655. But nine years later, the Dutch lost New Netherland to the British.

King Charles II granted New Netherland to his brother James, Duke of York. James renamed it New York. He gave the land between the Hudson and Delaware Rivers to Sir George Carteret and John Berkeley, 1st Baron Berkeley of Stratton. They named their colony New Jersey.

During the American Revolution (1775–1783), American and British armies clashed more than 100 times in New Jersey. The Battle of Trenton, fought on December 26, 1776, was a turning point in the war. In 1787, New Jersey became the third state.

In the 1800s and early 1900s, millions of European immigrants came to New Jersey in search of factory work. Today, more than 9 million New Jerseyans live in 7,354 square miles, making New Jersey the most densely populated state. Industry remains important. With thousands of farms, colonial-era homes and mills, and more than 100 miles of beaches, New Jersey is a small state of great diversity.

The 3rd State

Admitted to Union: December 18, 1787

Postal Abbreviation: NJ

Capital: Trenton

Nickname: Garden State

Population: 8,958,000

Land Area: 7,354 square miles (19,047 sq. km)

State Tree: Northern red oak

State Bird: Eastern goldfinch

Vacationers enjoy the sun and sand on Ocean City's boardwalk and beach.

43

New Mexico

Indians have lived in New Mexico for at least 10,000 years. One ancient group, the Puebloans, raised crops in the desert and built large stone dwellings on the cliffs and in the canyons.

Spanish explorers saw New Mexico for the first time in the early 1500s and tried to colonize it. But the land was isolated at the edge of the Spanish Empire, and the colony grew slowly. It became part of Mexico in 1821. When Mexico lost its northern land in the Mexican-American War in 1848, it was transferred to the U.S.

Confederate troops took over much of the territory at the start of the Civil War (1861–1865). The Union army recaptured it in 1862, and the following decades were a time of conflict. American newcomers and local Navajo made an uneasy peace in the late 1860s. But hostilities with some Apache continued until a prominent war leader, Geronimo, surrendered in 1886. Disputes among ranchers, homesteaders, and others erupted into violence in the 1870s and 1880s. Outlaws spread fear until federal lawmen established order.

New Mexico became a state in 1912. Since then, it has been a leader in nuclear and space research. The first atomic bombs were developed at Los Alamos in the early 1940s. And astronauts have trained for missions to space in New Mexico since the 1960s. Tourism is also important, as vacationers visit the state's spectacular deserts and mountains and rich Indian and Spanish cultural sites.

The 47th State

Admitted to Union: January 6, 1912

Postal Abbreviation: NM

Capital: Santa Fe

Nickname: Land of Enchantment

Population: 2,085,100

Land Area: 121,298 square miles (314,161 sq. km)

State Tree: Piñon pine

State Bird: Greater roadrunner

This multilevel pueblo is in Taos, New Mexico.

New York

New York was the home of the Iroquois and several Algonquian tribes when the first Europeans arrived. Italian explorer Giovanni da Verrazzano sailed into New York Bay in 1524. Henry Hudson explored the region for the Dutch in 1609. In 1624, the Dutch claimed the area and established their first permanent settlement at Fort Orange (now Albany). A year later, they bought what is now Manhattan from the Lenape Indians for 60 guilders (equal to $500 today) and founded New Amsterdam, today's New York City.

In 1664, the British captured New Netherland and renamed it New York. They occupied New York City during most of the American Revolution (1775–1783), and both the Americans and British sought to control the Hudson River, a key crossing point between New England and the rest of the colonies. Important battles took place in the state.

New York joined the Union in 1788. The opening of the Erie Canal in 1825 and the expansion of canal and railroad systems increased trade and helped industry grow. It also increased New York City's importance as a port and trade center. The arrival of millions of immigrants in New York City starting in the 1800s swelled the state's population. It also made the city a melting pot of many races and cultures.

Today, New York is a center of trade, finance, and communications. But the state still has huge areas of wilderness and many productive orchards and farms.

Niagara Falls lies on the border between New York and Canada.

The 11th State

Admitted to Union: July 26, 1788

Postal Abbreviation: NY

Capital: Albany

Nickname: Empire State

Population: 19,795,800

Land Area: 47,126 square miles (122,057 sq. km)

State Tree: Sugar maple

State Bird: Eastern bluebird

North Carolina

Cherokee and Tuscarora Indians, among others, were living in North Carolina when European explorers first saw the coast in the early 1500s. The English established their first colony in North America on Roanoke Island in 1585, but they left the following year. The English tried again, leaving a new group of settlers on the island in 1587. A few of them returned to England for supplies. When they came back in 1590, they found the colony had vanished. The fate of this "Lost Colony" remains a mystery.

In 1663, King Charles II granted the land of the large Carolina territory to eight proprietors, or businessmen. North Carolina became a separate colony in 1712. And after the American Revolution (1775–1783), the British lost their claims. In 1789, North Carolina became the 12th state of the new nation.

Although it was a slave state, North Carolina was reluctant to leave the Union during the Civil War (1861–1865). But after it eventually joined the Confederacy, the state provided the rebellion with more soldiers than any other.

In the early 1900s, North Carolina developed textile, furniture, and tobacco industries. These industries are still important, but North Carolinians also work in computers, banking, and tourism. The city of Charlotte is the second-largest banking center in the United States. And 28,000 acres of Cape Hatteras National Seashore draw visitors in search of nature and quiet time at the beach.

The 12th State

Admitted to Union: November 21, 1789

Postal Abbreviation: NC

Capital: Raleigh

Nickname: Tar Heel State

Population: 10,042,800

Land Area: 48,618 square miles (125,920 sq. km)

State Tree: Longleaf pine

State Bird: Northern cardinal

Bodie Island Lighthouse on Cape Hatteras National Seashore

North Dakota

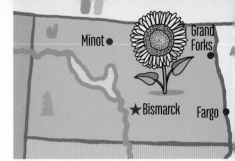

When French Canadian explorers crossed North Dakota in the 1730s, they found Mandan, Hidatsa, and Lakota Sioux Indians. France had already claimed much of the area in 1682 but didn't settle it. In 1803, France sold this land to the U.S. as part of the Louisiana Purchase.

The U.S. government encouraged homesteaders to move to the Dakota Territory in the 1860s. But it was hard to reach, and ongoing wars with Indians scared many white settlers. When the Northern Pacific Railway crossed the area in the 1870s, settlement picked up. By that time, local Indian tribes had been weakened by battles with the U.S. Army, and their primary food source, bison, had been hunted almost to extinction. When the Sioux, under Sitting Bull, surrendered in 1881, the peace that followed made the area more attractive to settlers.

The Dakota Territory was split into northern and southern sections in February 1889. That November, North Dakota became the 39th state. Farming expanded in the early 1900s, and the state passed laws to ease economic burdens on farmers and rural families.

In recent decades, oil extraction has played an important role in North Dakota's economy. But today, agriculture accounts for about 25% of jobs in the state—more than any other industry. Many North Dakotans farm or have jobs connected to agriculture. They continue to plow and plant the state's rich soil much as the first homesteaders did almost 150 years ago.

North Dakota's annual sunflower harvest is enough to produce 415 million bags of sunflower seeds.

The 39th State

Admitted to Union: November 2, 1889

Postal Abbreviation: ND

Capital: Bismarck

Nickname: Flickertail State

Population: 756,900

Land Area: 69,001 square miles (178,711 sq. km)

State Tree: American elm

State Bird: Western meadowlark

47

Ohio

French explorer René-Robert, sieur de La Salle was probably the first European to see Ohio, around 1669. The French and the British both claimed the area, which was home to the Iroquois Indians. But in 1763, the French lost most of their lands east of the Mississippi—including Ohio—to Britain.

After the American Revolution, in 1787, land north of the Ohio River and west of Pennsylvania became the Northwest Territory. War veterans established Marietta, the area's first permanent white settlement, a year later. But there were frequent clashes with American Indians who resented the takeover of their land. After the Battle of Fallen Timbers in 1794, they were forced to give up a large part of Ohio, and more settlers arrived to farm the fertile river valleys.

Ohio became a state in 1803. And after the Civil War ended in 1865, manufacturing and coal and iron ore industries expanded rapidly. Railroads and the Erie Canal—which linked Lake Erie with the Hudson River and the Atlantic Ocean—made it easier to ship products to eastern markets.

Foreign competition slowed some of Ohio's industries during the late 20th century. But Ohio remains a major Midwest industrial state, producing cars, chemicals, steel, processed food, and machinery. Tourism is also an important industry. Top attractions are Cuyahoga Valley National Park, located 20 miles south of Cleveland, and the Rock and Roll Hall of Fame, in downtown Cleveland.

The 17th State

Admitted to Union: March 1, 1803

Postal Abbreviation: OH

Capital: Columbus

Nickname: Buckeye State

Population: 11,613,400

Land Area: 40,861 square miles (105,829 sq. km)

State Tree: Ohio buckeye

State Bird: Northern cardinal

The Rock and Roll Hall of Fame brings visitors to Cleveland.

Oklahoma

From 500 to 1300 A.D., Oklahoma Indians known as mound builders lived a sophisticated life—until they mysteriously disappeared. The land was virtually free of people until Europeans began to enter the region. The state's recorded history began in 1541, when Spanish explorer Francisco Vásquez de Coronado came through on his quest for the "Lost City of Gold." The 1803 Louisiana Purchase made the land part of the U.S.

The land was officially set aside as Indian Territory in 1834. Since the 1820s, the Cherokee, Chickasaw, Creek, Choctaw, and Seminole tribes (called the Five Civilized Tribes by colonialists) had been forced to move there from the Southeastern U.S. The relocations required people to walk thousands of miles over land routes such as the Trail of Tears. The tribes suffered many hardships and losses along the way. They soon established themselves in their new home. When the western portion of the territory was opened to non-Indian settlers in 1889, thousands of people, including freed slaves, rushed to the area to stake claims to land.

When oil was discovered, statehood was assured. Newcomers flocked to the region to seek their fortunes, and Oklahoma joined the Union in 1907. Parts of the state suffered from severe drought during the Dust Bowl of the 1930s and 1940s. Today, oil, gas, and energy services still drive much of the state's industrial revenues, as do food processing and telecommunications.

Young dancers in native dress wait for a tribal ceremony to begin during a powwow. Today, there are 39 different Indian tribes headquartered in Oklahoma.

The 46th State

Admitted to Union: November 16, 1907

Postal Abbreviation: OK

State Tree: Eastern redbud

State Bird: Scissor-tailed flycatcher

Capital: Oklahoma City

Nickname: Sooner State

Population: 3,911,300

Land Area: 68,595 square miles (177,660 sq. km)

49

Oregon

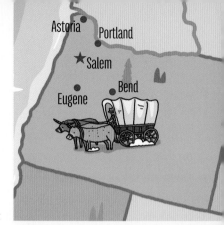

In the 1500s, Spanish and British explorers were the first Europeans to see Oregon. Francis Drake was the first European to come in contact with American Indians here in the 1570s. It wasn't until American sea captain Robert Gray reached the Columbia River in 1792, though, that Oregon became a significant stop for fur traders. At the time, Tillamook Indians were among the tribes living there.

In the early 1800s, Oregon Country stretched from Alaska to California. Several nations claimed it. All but the U.S. and Britain gave up claims by the 1820s.

The fur trade drew many of Oregon's first white settlers. Businessman John Jacob Astor established Astoria, the first American settlement west of the Rocky Mountains, in 1811. Settlers crossed North America in covered wagons in 1842 and 1843, traveling thousands of miles along the Oregon Trail to put down roots in the fertile Willamette Valley.

In 1846, Britain and the U.S. split the region (the land the British kept is now part of Canada). The Donation Land Act of 1850 gave free land to white males who agreed to come to Oregon to farm. Many native tribes were forced from their land at that time. Nine years later, Oregon became the 33rd state.

Today, Oregon's forests produce much of the nation's wood products. Farmers raise wheat and livestock, and fisheries are abundant. Oregon's natural beauty attracts vacationers, and the Portland metropolitan area is home to a booming tech sector, nicknamed Silicon Forest.

Mount Hood, an active volcano outside Portland, is Oregon's highest peak.

The 33rd State

Admitted to Union: February 14, 1859

Postal Abbreviation: OR

Capital: Salem

Nickname: Beaver State

Population: 4,029,000

Land Area: 95,988 square miles (248,608 sq. km)

State Tree: Douglas fir

State Bird: Western meadowlark

Pennsylvania

The earliest people of Pennsylvania included the Lenape and Nanticoke Indians. The first European to see Pennsylvania might have been the English explorer Henry Hudson, who sailed into Delaware Bay in 1609.

The Swedes established the area's first non-Indian settlement in the 1630s. The Dutch took over the Swedish colony in 1655. The British then removed the Dutch in 1664.

Soon, the British began to settle the colony. King Charles II owed money to William Penn's father, and he repaid it by granting Penn the land. Penn arrived in the colony in 1682. He was a Quaker, and he offered religious and political freedom to all settlers.

Pennsylvania played a key role in the nation's early history. The Declaration of Independence was written in Philadelphia in 1776. The U.S. Constitution was written there in 1787. Pennsylvania became the second state when it approved the new Constitution that December. Between 1790 and 1800, Philadelphia served as the U.S. capital.

In the early 1800s, Pennsylvania's resources—coal, oil, iron—boosted industry. The state remains an industrial center today, although new industries like medicine and technology have grown. Pennsylvania is home to the world's largest chocolate and candy factory in the town of Hershey. But it is also an area of green pastures and cornfields. Its covered bridges, quaint villages, and 200-year-old homes are reminders of the state's historic past.

The 2nd State

Admitted to Union: December 12, 1787

Postal Abbreviation: PA

Capital: Harrisburg

Nickname: Keystone State

Population: 12,802,500

Land Area: 44,743 square miles (115,883 sq. km)

State Tree: Eastern hemlock

State Bird: Ruffed grouse

Independence Hall, Philadelphia. John Hancock, president of the Second Continental Congress, signed the Declaration of Independence here on July 4, 1776.

Rhode Island

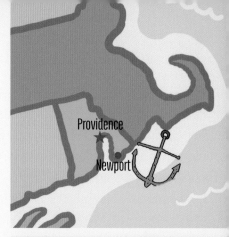

Narragansett and Wampanoag Indians lived in Rhode Island for thousands of years before Italian explorer Giovanni da Verrazzano saw its shore in 1524. In the 1600s, it became a haven for independent people with unpopular ideas. The leaders of the Massachusetts Bay Colony expelled Roger Williams, a defender of religious freedom, for disagreeing with their rules. He headed south to Narragansett Bay. There, Williams founded Rhode Island's first permanent European settlement, near today's Providence, in 1636.

When the American Revolution began in 1775, hundreds of citizens volunteered to fight. After independence was won, Rhode Island was the last of the original 13 colonies to approve the U.S. Constitution. It joined the Union in 1790—but only after a promise that a Bill of Rights would be added to the Constitution. The Bill of Rights—the first 10 amendments—includes freedom of speech and of religion.

The textile industry began in Rhode Island in the late 1700s, when America's first water-powered cotton mill was built in Pawtucket. The nation's jewelry industry began in Rhode Island in the 1790s. The state remained a leader in these industries well into the 20th century.

Narragansett Bay has been an important shipbuilding and trade center in Rhode Island since the 1700s. Today, it shows Rhode Island's unique ocean character, with naval facilities, shipping, fishing, and other water activities. At 37 miles wide and 48 miles long, Rhode Island is the smallest state in the country.

The 13th State

Admitted to Union: May 29, 1790

Postal Abbreviation: RI

State Tree: Red maple

State Bird: Rhode Island Red hen

Capital: Providence

Nickname: Ocean State

Population: 1,056,300

Land Area: 1,034 square miles (2,678 sq. km)

Providence County Courthouse

52

South Carolina

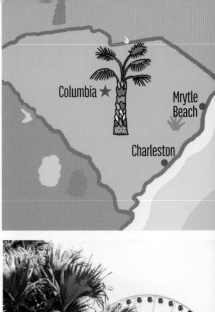

The Spanish were the first Europeans to explore the South Carolina coast in 1521, but they failed to establish permanent settlements. And though Cherokee, Catawba, and other Indians already lived there, the English were eager for a foothold in the area. In 1663, King Charles II gave a parcel of land, which included today's South Carolina, to eight friends. They established the first permanent European settlement near Charleston in 1670.

South Carolina became a separate colony in 1729 and grew wealthy from rice and indigo crops, which were used to make ink. After the American Revolution, in 1788, South Carolina ratified the U.S. Constitution and joined the new nation as the eighth state.

The state's economy was based on large plantations worked by slaves. When Abraham Lincoln was elected president in 1860, some plantation owners feared slavery would end. In December 1860, South Carolina became the first state to leave the Union. Months later, on April 12, 1861, Confederate soldiers fired on Charleston's Fort Sumter, touching off the Civil War.

Textile mills provided jobs in the late 1800s and early 1900s. After cotton crops were destroyed by insects called boll weevils in the 1920s, farmers began to grow tobacco and fruit. About two-thirds of South Carolina is covered in forest. Forestry and lumber are the largest industries in the state. South Carolina also manufactures aircraft, autos, and plastics. Its warm climate and sandy beaches draw tourists.

Myrtle Beach is a 312-acre state park.

The 8th State

Admitted to Union: May 23, 1788

Postal Abbreviation: SC

Capital: Columbia

Nickname: Palmetto State

Population: 4,896,150

Land Area: 30,061 square miles (77,857 sq. km)

State Tree: Sabal palm

State Birds: Carolina wren, wild turkey

South Dakota

Rapid City • ★ Pierre

Sioux Falls •

Before white settlers arrived, South Dakota was home to Cheyenne and Arikara Indians. The Lakota Sioux joined them in the 17th and 18th centuries, when rival tribes and white settlers pushed them west from Minnesota.

The first Europeans to travel through South Dakota, the Verendrye brothers, claimed the land for France. South Dakota became American soil when the U.S. bought French Louisiana in 1803. The first permanent settlement, Fort Pierre, was founded in 1817.

In the early 1800s, most South Dakota settlers were connected with the fur trade and lived along the Missouri River. But land disputes with the Sioux caused frequent fighting. A treaty gave the Indians most of the region west of the river and brought peace for a while. But whites violated the agreement when gold was discovered in the Black Hills in the 1870s. Prospectors poured into the Indians' sacred land.

In 1889, the Dakota Territory was divided into north and south. Soon after, North and South Dakota entered the Union. The following year, hundreds of Sioux were killed near Wounded Knee. The state opened more Indian land to white settlement and distributed it by lottery.

Today, South Dakota is home to Badlands National Park, 244,000 acres of protected land that surround a rich deposit of prehistoric fossils. Tourism is a billion-dollar business, but farming and agriculture remain important to the state's economy.

Mount Rushmore National Memorial is a massive sculpture. Its roughly 60-foot-high granite faces depict U.S. presidents George Washington, Thomas Jefferson, Theodore Roosevelt, and Abraham Lincoln.

The 40th State

Admitted to Union: November 2, 1889

Postal Abbreviation: SD

Capital: Pierre

Nickname: Mount Rushmore State

Population: 858,500

Land Area: 75,811 square miles (196,350 sq. km)

State Tree: Black Hills spruce (white spruce)

State Bird: Ring-necked pheasant

Tennessee

Cherokee and Chickasaw Indians inhabited Tennessee's mountains and river valleys for centuries before Europeans arrived. The Spanish explorer Hernando de Soto traveled the region in 1540, and French settlement began in the early 1700s.

The British claimed the area in 1763, after the French and Indian War. Eastern Tennessee was then part of North Carolina. But after the American Revolution, in 1784, North Carolina gave that land to the federal government as payment for war debt. The people who lived there did not like this, and they decided to form their own country, Franklin. It disbanded three years later. In 1790, Tennessee became a separate U.S. territory. It joined the Union in 1796.

The people of Tennessee did not agree on the issue of slavery. Even so, the state joined the Confederacy in 1861 at the start of the Civil War. The Confederacy was made up of pro-slavery southern states. In 1862, Union forces made up of anti-slavery northern states won the Battle of Shiloh against the Confederate Army. After the war, Tennessee was the first state to rejoin the Union.

The city of Nashville is an influential center of the country music industry. But Tennessee is a largely industrial state. Chemical processing, electronic machinery, electrical power, and textile production are important to the state's economy. Farming is less central to the economy than it was in the past, but beef cattle remains a major industry, and tobacco is still Tennessee's most important crop.

The 16th State

Admitted to Union: June 1, 1796

Postal Abbreviation: TN

Capital: Nashville

Nickname: Volunteer State

Population: 6,600,300

Land Area: 41,235 square miles (106,798 sq. km)

State Tree: Tulip poplar

State Birds: Northern mockingbird, bobwhite quail

Nashville, Tennessee, is America's country music capital.

Texas

Caddo, Comanche, Kiowa, and other Indians lived in Texas when Spanish explorer Álvar Núñez Cabeza de Vaca arrived in the 1520s. By the early 1700s, the Spanish had built forts and religious settlements, called missions, in the area. It was the northern frontier of New Spain, which included Mexico.

Mexico won its independence from Spain in 1821. That same year, Stephen F. Austin, known as the father of Texas, led 3,000 American families to the region. Others followed, attracted by the fertile soil. The Mexican government forbade American immigration in 1830, but settlers continued to come.

In December 1835, during Texas's war for independence from Mexico, 200 Texan volunteers seized the Alamo, an old mission chapel in San Antonio. The volunteers defended it for 13 days against thousands of soldiers led by the Mexican general Antonio López de Santa Anna. In 1836, Texas forces led by commander Sam Houston defeated Santa Anna and his army near what is today the city of Houston. Texas became an independent republic. After nine years, it became a state, in 1845.

The discovery of oil near Beaumont in 1901 began an oil boom. After World War II, the aerospace and electronics industries expanded. Today, Texas is the nation's biggest producer of oil, cattle, sheep, minerals, and cotton. It is a modern, industrial state with a diverse population. Three of its major cities—Houston, San Antonio, and Dallas—boast populations greater than one million.

The 28th State

Admitted to Union: December 29, 1845

Postal Abbreviation: TX

Capital: Austin

Nickname: Lone Star State

Population: 27,469,100

Land Area: 261,232 square miles (676,587 sq. km)

State Tree: Pecan

State Bird: Northern mockingbird

Mexican Americans riding at a charreada tournament at a ranch in South Texas. A charreada is similar to a rodeo.

Utah

When Spanish explorers Silvestre Vélez de Escalante and Francisco Atanasio Domínguez arrived in the late 1700s, the Ute, Paiute, and Shoshone Indians were living in Utah. A religious group, the Mormons, established the first permanent white settlements in the area in 1847. They set up farms and used irrigation to grow crops in the dry climate. At the time, the land was part of Mexico, but it became U.S. territory in 1848 after the Mexican-American War.

The Mormons applied for statehood in 1850 and again in 1856, but the U.S. Congress rejected the bids because of the group's practice of polygamy, or multiple marriages. In 1869, the final spike for the first transcontinental railroad was driven at Promontory Point, opening Utah and all the western states. Settlement expanded throughout the area around the Great Salt Lake, in the Wasatch Range. Finally, in 1896, Utah became a state.

In the early 1900s, the U.S. government helped develop irrigation projects, which opened up more farmland. Transportation networks grew, giving farms and mines better access to markets. Gold and silver mines in the Bingham Canyon increased production, as did copper and coal mines.

Today, Utah is still rich in natural resources. But high-tech industry, and the government and transportation industries, are also important. The state's mountains, canyons, and colorful, flat-topped hills (called mesas) attract tourists from around the world.

The State Capitol overlooks Salt Lake City.

The 45th State

Admitted to Union: January 4, 1896

Postal Abbreviation: UT

Capital: Salt Lake City

Nickname: Beehive State

Population: 2,995,900

Land Area: 82,170 square miles (212,818 sq. km)

State Tree: Quaking aspen

State Bird: California seagull

Vermont

Iroquois and Algonquian tribes lived in Vermont before European settlement. French explorer Samuel de Champlain visited the area in 1609. But Vermont's first permanent European settlement, a British outpost known as Fort Dummer (near today's Brattleboro), wasn't founded until 1724.

Land disputes raged in Vermont during the mid-1700s. Officials in New Hampshire and New York granted the same pieces of Vermont land to different settlers. The British government sided with the New Yorkers. But settlers with New Hampshire grants refused to give up their land. They organized themselves into a group called the Green Mountain Boys and forced out many of the New Yorkers.

During the American Revolution (1775–1783), the Green Mountain Boys turned their attention to fighting the British. They captured Fort Ticonderoga in 1775, and in 1777, Vermont declared itself an independent republic. Its constitution made slavery illegal. Independence lasted until 1791, when Vermont became the 14th state.

In the early 1800s, Vermont's wool industry prospered. But competition from the West caused Vermont farmers to switch from sheep to dairy farming—which is still important in the state today.

Industry never became dominant in Vermont, and the state has kept its rural character. Residents and tourists enjoy Vermont's quaint farms and villages, forested hillsides, and clear mountain streams.

The 14th State

Admitted to Union: March 4, 1791

Postal Abbreviation: VT

Capital: Montpelier

Nickname: Green Mountain State

Population: 626,050

Land Area: 9,217 square miles (23,871 sq. km)

State Tree: Sugar maple

State Bird: Hermit thrush

Autumn countryside in the Green Mountains

Virginia

Powhatan and Cherokee Indians inhabited Virginia long before English colonization. In 1607, the first permanent English settlement in North America was established at Jamestown. In 1624, England made Virginia its first New World colony. Settlers struggled in the beginning. But they soon learned to grow food and raise tobacco, which they exported to Europe.

Virginians played important roles in early American history. Thomas Jefferson wrote the Declaration of Independence. George Washington commanded the Continental Army during the American Revolution. Many important battles were fought in Virginia. The British surrender, which ended the war, took place at Yorktown in 1781. Afterward, James Madison, a Virginian, helped to write the U.S. Constitution. In 1788, Virginia approved the Constitution and became the 10th state.

In the early 1800s, slave-dependent plantations expanded in Eastern Virginia. When the Civil War began in 1861, Virginia seceded from the Union. But several western counties stayed loyal to the Union. These separated from Virginia to form West Virginia.

In the late 1800s and early 1900s, the state's tobacco, textile, and shipbuilding industries grew. The state is home to many who work in the District of Columbia, and the U.S. government plays a large part in its economy. Tourism is important, too. Visitors tour sites that preserve Virginia's history, such as Monticello, the home of Thomas Jefferson.

Monticello, the home of Thomas Jefferson, the third U.S. President and author of the Declaration of Independence

The 10th State

Admitted to Union: June 25, 1788

Postal Abbreviation: VA

Capital: Richmond

Nickname: Old Dominion

Population: 8,383,000

Land Area: 39,490 square miles (102,279 sq. km)

State Tree: Flowering dogwood

State Bird: Northern cardinal

Washington

Before Spanish and English explorers sailed along its coast in the 1500s, Washington was home to Indian tribes such as the Cayuse, Nez Percé, and Yakima. Several European expeditions came through in the early 1800s, looking for the Northwest Passage, a water route from the Atlantic to the Pacific. The Passage proved to be a fantasy, but the area's rich animal life attracted American and British fur trappers and traders.

Both the U.S. and Britain claimed Washington in the early 1800s. At the time, the land was part of Oregon Territory. In 1846, the two countries agreed on how to divide the land. And in 1853, Congress created Washington Territory out of the northern part of Oregon Territory.

Settlement increased in the 1860s when gold was discovered near Walla Walla. The Northern Pacific Railroad, which connected the region to the East in 1883, also spurred population growth. Washington became a state in 1889. By that time, agriculture was booming in the fertile valleys. The state is home to Mount St. Helens, a volcano that last erupted in 1980, triggering the largest recorded landslide on earth. Olympic National Park, in the northwestern corner of the state, includes temperate rain forest and towering mountains.

Today, Washington's snowcapped mountains and lush forests attract tourists. Its eastern farmlands produce wheat—and more apples and pears than any other state. The state's largest city, Seattle, is a center for high-tech industry.

The 42nd State

Admitted to Union: November 11, 1889

Postal Abbreviation: WA

Capital: Olympia

Nickname: Evergreen State

Population: 7,170,350

Land Area: 66,456 square miles (172,119 sq. km)

State Tree: Western hemlock

State Bird: Willow goldfinch

A girl enjoys the outdoors in one of Washington's many forests.

West Virginia

West Virginia was originally part of Virginia, which became a state in 1788. The first settlers crossed the Appalachian Mountains into the region in the 1700s, where they joined Indian tribes such as the Iroquois and the Shawnee.

From the start, there were important differences within Virginia. Wealthy, slaveholding plantation owners dominated the East. The mountainous west was an area of small family farms. At the start of the Civil War, in 1861, Virginia seceded from the Union, which was made up of anti-slavery northern states. But 40 western counties opposed this action. They set up their own government at Wheeling in 1861 to support the Union. In 1863, they joined the Union as the state of West Virginia.

The state thrived by tapping its natural reserves of saltpeter, needed to manufacture gunpowder during the war, and later coal, which powered industry throughout the East.

The building of railroads in the late 1800s boosted industries based on West Virginia's resources. Violent clashes occurred in the late 1800s and early 1900s between mine owners and workers struggling for better conditions, higher pay, and the right to join unions.

New energy sources reduced the demand for coal after World War II, and machines reduced the need for miners. Many people left the state in search of work. Today, West Virginia is looking to industrial growth and tourism to provide new opportunities for its people.

Blackwater Falls State Park

The 35th State

Admitted to Union: June 20, 1863

Capital: Charleston

Nickname: Mountain State

Population: 1,844,100

Land Area: 24,038 square miles (62,259 sq. km)

State Tree: Sugar maple

State Bird: Northern cardinal

Wisconsin

Winnebago Indians farmed, hunted, and fished in Wisconsin when French explorer Jean Nicolet arrived in the 1630s. Fur trappers and missionaries followed. Abundant wildlife made this highly forested land desirable to both the French and the British, who sought to expand resources for the fur trade. Britain conquered much of the land during the French and Indian War, and it was given to England in the Treaty of Paris, which ended that war in 1763. After the American Revolution (1775–1783), the land became part of the U.S.

Large numbers of people came to Wisconsin in the 1820s, when rich lead deposits were discovered in the Southwest. (Because some of the miners lived in shelters dug into the hills, people called them badgers, after an animal that lives in underground burrows.) People from the Eastern U.S. settled in the area after traveling to nearby Illinois along the Erie Canal. By 1836, Wisconsin had become a U.S. territory. It gained statehood in 1848. One of the most important political movements in U.S. history, progressivism, began in Wisconsin in the late 1890s and early 1900s. Progressives passed laws that regulated businesses, gave more power to ordinary people, and protected workers. Many of these reforms later spread to other states and the national government.

Most of the people of Wisconsin work in services and industry. Electrical manufacturing, paper mills, and manufacturing rank high on the list of industries in the state. But it is also a leader in the production of dairy products.

The 30th State

Admitted to Union: May 29, 1848

Postal Abbreviation: WI

Capital: Madison

Nickname: Badger State

Population: 5,771,300

Land Area: 54,158 square miles (140,268 sq. km)

State Tree: Sugar maple

State Bird: American robin

A Green Bay Packers football fan is called a cheesehead.

Wyoming

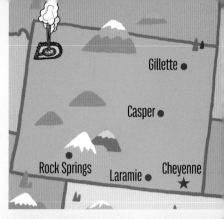

Arapaho, Crow, Cheyenne, and other Indian tribes have inhabited Wyoming's expansive lands for thousands of years. White settlers arrived only about 200 years ago. Much of Wyoming became U.S. territory with the 1803 Louisiana Purchase. Soon after, American fur trappers and traders established trading posts that became important towns, such as Laramie.

During the mid-1800s, several of the most important trails to the west—the Oregon Trail, the California Trail, and the Mormon Trail—cut across the region. Thousands of settlers came through. But few chose to stay on Wyoming's dry eastern plains or in its high mountains.

In the late 1800s, several events increased Wyoming's population. Gold was discovered, and railroad lines were built across the state. Cattle ranching began. People were also attracted to the natural beauty of Yellowstone, the first U.S. national park, created by President Theodore Roosevelt in 1872. In 1890, Wyoming became the 44th state.

In the 20th century, irrigation projects brought power and water to isolated towns and farms. Oil, uranium, and coal provided needed resources—and jobs. Wyoming has few people and a harsh environment. But that environment has attracted tourists, who support the state's economy. Almost half of the state is owned by the federal government, which employs people in national parks and forest management. Wyoming's vast plains, rugged mountains, rodeos, and ranches provide visitors with a taste of the Old West.

Castle Geyser shoots hot water in Yellowstone National Park.

The 44th State

Admitted to Union: July 10, 1890

Postal Abbreviation: WY

Capital: Cheyenne

Nickname: Equality State

Population: 586,100

Land Area: 97,093 square miles (251,470 sq. km)

State Tree: Plains cottonwood

State Bird: Western meadowlark

THE FEDERAL DISTRICT:
Washington, D.C.

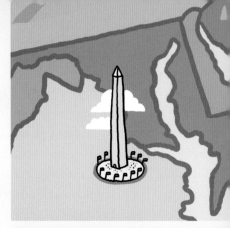

When the American colonies declared independence from Britain in 1776, they did so from Philadelphia, Pennsylvania, then the capital of the young nation. New York, New York, also served as the capital for a short period of time. But the authors of the U.S. Constitution wanted the capital city to be independent from any of the states. So in 1790, the U.S. Congress passed the Residence Act, which approved the creation of the national capital.

President George Washington picked a site for the city at the junction of the Potomac and Anacostia Rivers, filled with farmland, wetland, and forest. Originally part of the state of Maryland, and bordering Virginia to the south, the area was turned over to the federal government. By 1800, Washington, District of Columbia—named after George Washington and Christopher Columbus—was declared the capital of the United States of America.

In 1791, President Washington hired the French engineer Pierre Charles L'Enfant to plan the city. L'Enfant completed his draft of the city very quickly. But many of his colleagues found him difficult to work with, so Washington fired him the following year. A group of surveyors led by Major Andrew Ellicott, which included a free African American amateur astronomer named Benjamin Banneker, laid out the borders of the city as L'Enfant's plan intended. By the end of 1800, Congress had held its first session in the city, and President John Adams was living in the White House.

Admitted to Union: July 16, 1790

Tree: Scarlet oak

Postal Abbreviation: DC

Bird: Wood thrush

Capital: none

Nickname: Federal City

Population: 672,228

Land Area: 61 square miles (158 sq. km)

The Lincoln Memorial is located on the National Mall in Washington, D.C.

Residents of Washington, D.C., have been able to vote for president only since 1961, when the 23rd Amendment to the U.S. Constitution was passed. And Washingtonians still couldn't vote for their own local officials until 1974. This is because most voting laws are controlled by state governments, not the federal government. Because Washington is on federal and not state lands, there were no specific laws laying out the voting rights of its residents. Residents of the capital are still the only American citizens who have no representatives in Congress.

Unlike most large American cities, like New York or Chicago, Washington, D.C., has no skyscrapers and very little industry. The nation's capital and its residents are almost entirely dedicated to governing the nation. Most residents who do not work for the federal government work either in education, tourism, news media—which reports mostly on the government—or for one of the city's many museums and monuments, which are dedicated to the history of the U.S. and its people.

Most of the capital's famous museums and monuments—including the Lincoln Memorial, dedicated to President Abraham Lincoln; the Washington Monument, an obelisk commemorating George Washington; and the Smithsonian National Air and Space Museum—are located on or around the National Mall, a national park in the downtown area of the city.

The Washington Monument

The Thomas Jefferson Memorial

The Dr. Martin Luther King, Jr. Memorial

U.S Territories and Commonwealths

The U.S. owns a number of islands, called territories or commonwealths, that are not among the 50 states. Of the 16 official U.S. territories and commonwealths, only five are permanently inhabited, with the rest serving as military facilities, research stations, or wildlife preserves.

In all of the territories except for American Samoa, the inhabitants are considered American citizens. Samoans are not automatically citizens at birth but can enter the U.S. at any time.

Several U.S. territories control their local governments, and U.S. commonwealths control most of their own internal affairs. However, American officials have a say in how the territories and commonwealths are governed, and both rely on the U.S. for military protection, economic aid, and most foreign affairs. Each territory sends a nonvoting delegate or resident commissioner to the House of Representatives.

INHABITED TERRITORIES AND COMMONWEALTHS

American Samoa

The U.S. established control over the Samoan islands in the early 1900s. The people of American Samoa are not U.S. citizens but can enter and leave the country without restrictions, in order to work, attend school, or live.

Status: Territory

Capital: Pago Pago

Population: 66,000 (2010 U.S. Census); most people are Polynesian

Geography: Seven tiny islands in the South Pacific about 2,300 miles (3,700 km) southwest of Hawaii; 76 square miles (198 sq. km)

Economy: Fishing, tuna canning

Camel Rock near the village of Lauli'i, American Samoa

Guam

Guam was turned over to the U.S. by Spain in 1898, at the end of the Spanish-American War. The U.S. built military bases in Guam after World War II.

Talofofo Falls, Guam

Status: Territory

Capital: Hagåtña

Population: 181,000 (2010 U.S. Census); mostly native Chamorro (descendants of the original inhabitants from Southeast Asia) and Filipino

Geography: Island in the western Pacific; 210 square miles (543 sq. km)

Economy: Tourism, U.S. military bases, fishing, and handicrafts

Northern Mariana Islands

The U.S. took the Northern Mariana Islands from Japan during World War II. In 1947, the United Nations gave the U.S. control over the islands and two other Micronesian island groups, the Marshall Islands and the Caroline Islands. The Northern Marianas chose to become a U.S. commonwealth in 1975.

Status: Commonwealth

Capital: Saipan

Population: 48,000 (2010 U.S. Census); mostly Asian and Pacific Islanders

Geography: A group of 16 western Pacific islands south of Japan and east of the Philippines; 182 square miles (472 sq. km)

Economy: Tourism, government employment, textiles, farming, and fishing

Bell tower of a seaside chapel on the island of Saipan, Northern Mariana Islands

U.S. Virgin Islands

Denmark first established settlements on the Virgin Islands in the 1600s and early 1700s and controlled them until they were sold to the U.S. in 1917.

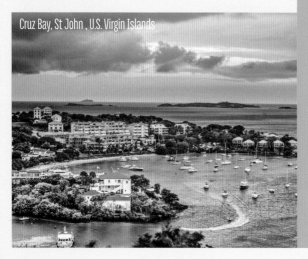

Cruz Bay, St John , U.S. Virgin Islands

Status: Territory

Capital: Charlotte Amalie

Population: 110,000 (2010 U.S. Census); mostly West Indian

Geography: A group of three main islands—St. Thomas, St. John, St. Croix—between the Atlantic Ocean and the Caribbean Sea; 134 square miles (249 sq. km)

Economy: Tourism, government employment, oil refining, aluminum ore (bauxite) refining, rum production

Puerto Rico

Puerto Rico's first inhabitants were the Taino Indians, who originally came from South America. Christopher Columbus reached the islands in 1493 and claimed them in the name of the Spanish Empire. But serious settlement didn't really begin until 1898, when the Spanish gave the island to the U.S.

Puerto Rico became a U.S. territory in 1917 and a commonwealth on July 25, 1952. It is the largest and most important of the U.S. territories and commonwealths.

Puerto Ricans have voted several times since 1967 on whether to seek statehood. Islanders are split on the issue. Still, a majority of citizens have voted to maintain Puerto Rico's commonwealth status. As an unincorporated territory, Puerto Rico sends a nonvoting resident commissioner to the House of Representatives.

Status: Commonwealth

Capital: San Juan

Population: 3,979,000 (2010 U.S. Census)

Geography: One main island and two smaller islands located about 1,000 miles (1,600 km) southwest of Miami between the Atlantic Ocean and the Caribbean Sea; 3,424 square miles (8,868 sq. km)

Economy: Clothing, prescription drugs, tourism

A sentry box of Fort San Felipe del Morro in old San Juan, Puerto Rico

Northern Mariana Islands
Wake Island
Midway Islands
Johnston Atoll
Guam
Howland Island
Baker Island
Kingman Reef
Palmyra Atoll
Jarvis Island
American Samoa
Navassa Island
Serranilla Bank
Bajo Nuevo Bank
Puerto Rico
U.S. Virgin Islands

Uninhabited Territories, Commonwealths, and Possessions

Bajo Nuevo Bank

Baker Island

Howland Island

Jarvis Island

Johnston Atoll

Kingman Reef

Midway Islands

Navassa Island

Palmyra Atoll

Serranilla Bank

Wake Island

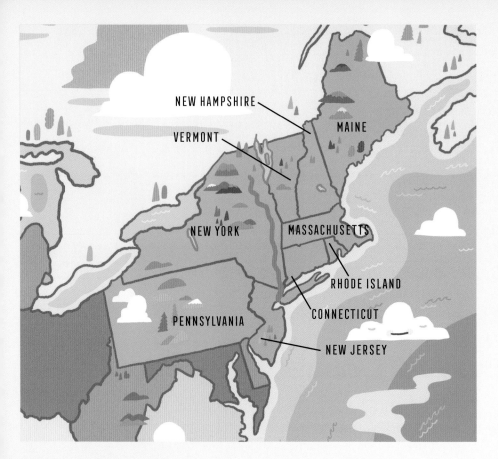

The Northeast

The Northeast portion of the U.S. consists of New England—Maine, Vermont, New Hampshire, Rhode Island, Massachusetts, and Connecticut—and the Mid-Atlantic states—New York, Pennsylvania, and New Jersey. Each of these states, with the exceptions of Maine and Vermont, was one of the original 13 colonies.

The climate in the Northeast is mild and coastal, with cold, snowy winters and warm, wet summers. Most of the major cities in the Northeast are located near water and were originally supported by fishing, shipping, and travel. This includes oceanside cities such as New York, New York, and Boston, Massachusetts, and riverside cities such as Philadelphia and Pittsburgh, Pennsylvania, which was called the Gateway to the West during America's westward expansion.

As technology improved during the 1800s, these cities became centers of industry, with factories that manufactured products as diverse as clothing, steel, books, and jewelry. Many of the surrounding areas were heavily forested and rich with natural resources, including trees for lumber, animals such as deer and beaver for fur, and coal for fuel. The waterways that connected the cities were used to transport the goods produced in and around them to other cities, both in the Northeast and across the country. Much of the manufacturing that supported the Northeast eventually left the region, resulting in the loss of many jobs. Many states in the Northeast, including New York and Pennsylvania, fall into an area that is sometimes referred to as the Rust Belt.

The Northeast occupies some of the first lands to be settled in the U.S., and its major cities, especially New York and Boston, became home for some of the country's earliest wealthy and intellectual families. Because of this, the area is full of old and established universities, as well as industries that focus on the spread of information, like publishing and news media.

The Northeast is also the most densely populated region in America, with an average of almost 350 people per square mile, making it two and a half times more densely populated than the second-most populous region, the South. The New York metropolitan area, which includes Southern New York, Long Island, Northern New Jersey, Southern Connecticut, and a small slice of Northeastern Pennsylvania, is by far the most populous in the country.

The Statue of Liberty in New York Harbor, New York

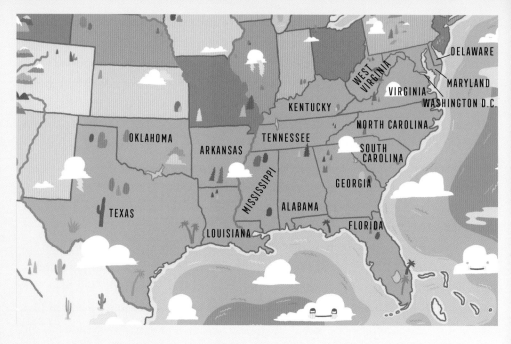

The South

The South is the second-most densely populated region in the U.S., behind the Northeast. The first area to be colonized by the British in what would become the United States of America was the Commonwealth of Virginia. Five other Southern states—Delaware, Maryland, South Carolina, North Carolina, and Georgia—were among the first 13 colonies.

The remainder of the Southern states, most of which were added to the U.S. during the 75 years following the signing of the Declaration of Independence, are Florida, West Virginia, Alabama, Kentucky, Mississippi, Tennessee, Arkansas, Louisiana, Oklahoma, and Texas. Washington, D.C., is also part of the South.

Some of the South is rainy and swampy, and some of it is dry and dusty, but aside from its mountain ranges and its most northern areas, all of it is hot. In wetter regions, this makes for excellent agriculture, and the South is one of the largest producers of fruits, vegetables, rice, cotton, and domestic animals. Some industries in the South are localized; Virginia, for example, grows the bulk of the nation's tobacco, while Texas—mostly hot and dry but very spacious—is the Southern state known for raising the most cattle.

Because it is home to Washington, D.C., the South is where many of our federal government's employees live and work. Virginia, just next door to the capital, is sometimes called the Mother of Presidents because eight U.S. presidents were born there, more than in any other state in the country.

Much of the South is called the Bible Belt. This is because the South has a high population of evangelical Christians, and Christian values often influence the region's politics and culture.

During the Civil War, most of the South fought against much of the Northern states in an attempt to secede, or separate, from the U.S.

The Midwest

The middle region of the U.S., the Midwest, extends from Ohio to Nebraska. Made up of Ohio, Indiana, Michigan, Wisconsin, Illinois, Minnesota, Missouri, Iowa, Kansas, Nebraska, and North and South Dakota, it is a mostly flat territory, filled with rivers, lakes, and long stretches of fields, farms, and prairies.

On its eastern and northern edges, much of the climate is similar to the Northeast—cold in winter and warm in the summer, with seasonal rain and snow. Missouri is closer in climate to the Southern states—warm much of the year, with mild winters and wet, humid summers. The westernmost states, including Kansas, Iowa, Nebraska, and the Dakotas, are much drier, with cold winters and strong winds that blow across the flat landscape.

The Midwest includes much of the Great Plains, a region that runs from Montana in the West to Texas in the South, and occupies most of the Dakotas, Nebraska, and Kansas. The Great Plains has been called America's Breadbasket because its flat grasslands and rolling prairies make it an excellent place to grow grains such as wheat. It is also home to a number of America's indigenous tribes; some of the best-known American Indians, such as Crazy Horse, are from the Great Plains. The iconic bison, also called the American buffalo, makes its home in the Great Plains.

Parts of the Midwest, including Ohio, Indiana, Michigan, and Illinois, are also part of the Rust Belt, which stretches through some of the Northeast and a little bit of the South. These are areas where companies that manufactured products including steel, cars, and industrial machinery used to be based. Some of those companies, like Ford and General Motors in Detroit, Michigan, are still based in the Midwest, but much of the actual manufacturing is now done overseas, which left many in the region without jobs.

America's "Corn Belt," which takes up much of Minnesota, Illinois, Indiana, Wisconsin, and Iowa, is also part of the Midwest. This area is filled with farms and is where most of the corn in our country is grown. Much of the famous Mississippi River also borders states in the Midwest, making those states—including Minnesota and Missouri—important for shipping and travel.

The West

The American West, the largest geographic region in the country, is a land of extremes. The southern portion, consisting of Arizona, New Mexico, and much of Nevada and Utah, is filled with mountain ranges and deserts. The northern portion, which includes Western Montana and Northern Idaho, is a rainy region filled with thick forests. In the central portion, made up of Colorado, Wyoming, Idaho, and some of Montana, mountains, including the famous Rocky Mountains, span much of the land.

Because the West is so vast, its climate varies, from the hot and dry year-round temperatures of its southwest portion to the wet and cool year-round temperatures of its northwest portion, and everything in between. Much of the West's industry comes from tourism. The region is packed to the brim with national parks, including Yellowstone and the Grand Canyon, and its mountainous regions make for great skiing and snowboarding.

The Pacific States

The Pacific States include Alaska, Hawaii, Oregon, Washington, and California. California grows much of America's produce in its central portion—sometimes called the Salad Belt because of its large yields of leafy greens like lettuce and fruits like tomatoes, oranges, grapes, and lemons. It is wet and cool up north and hot and dry down south. California is also known for its excellent surfing and is home to most of the American film business, the state's most influential industry. Its booming technology and Internet sector takes up much of the real estate in Silicon Valley, south of San Francisco. Many technology companies also operate in cities like Seattle, Washington, and Portland, Oregon.

Far up north is the snowy and mountainous Alaska, and to the west, in the middle of the Pacific Ocean, lies the tropical volcanic islands of Hawaii, the only state in the Union not attached to the North American continent.

The Golden Gate Bridge in San Francisco, California

Explore Some More

STATE GOVERNMENTS

You can learn more about each of the 50 states by visiting the official sites of their governments.

Alabama alabama.gov

Alaska alaska.gov

Arizona az.gov

Arkansas arkansas.gov

California ca.gov

Colorado colorado.gov

Connecticut ct.gov

Delaware delaware.gov

Florida myflorida.com

Georgia georgia.gov

Hawaii hawaii.gov

Idaho idaho.gov

Illinois illinois.gov

Indiana in.gov

Iowa iowa.gov

Kansas kansas.gov

Kentucky kentucky.gov

Louisiana louisiana.gov

Maine maine.gov

Maryland maryland.gov

Massachusetts mass.gov

Michigan michigan.gov

Minnesota mn.gov

Mississippi ms.gov

Missouri mo.gov

Montana mt.gov

Nebraska nebraska.gov

Nevada nv.gov

New Hampshire nh.gov

New Jersey newjersey.gov

New Mexico newmexico.gov

New York ny.gov

North Carolina nc.gov

North Dakota nd.gov

Ohio ohio.gov

Oklahoma ok.gov

Oregon oregon.gov

Pennsylvania pa.gov

Rhode Island ri.gov

South Carolina sc.gov

South Dakota sd.gov

Tennessee tn.gov

Texas texas.gov

Utah utah.gov

Vermont vermont.gov

Virginia virginia.gov

Washington wa.gov

West Virginia wv.gov

Wisconsin wisconsin.gov

Wyoming wyo.gov

National Congress of American Indians *ncai.org*

The National Congress of American Indians is the oldest and biggest organization dedicated to the tribal people who have lived here for thousands of years.

State historical societies *preservationdirectory.com*

State historical societies work to preserve the history of individual states. They can often provide primary sources (letters, diaries, and memoirs written by historical figures) and true stories about each state.

Index

Picture Credits